UNDER THE SUN

Sapphire Cay, book 2

RJ SCOTT

MEREDITH RUSSELL

Love Lane Books

Copyright

All Rights Reserved

Dedication

For our family and friends

SAPPHIRE CAY 2

UNDER THE *Sun*

RJ SCOTT & MEREDITH RUSSELL

Chapter One

"HOW LONG'S IT BEEN SINCE YOU'VE VISITED THE CAY?"

Jamie Durand lifted his head as the thirty-minute silence was finally broken, and he turned his attention to the tall, tanned man steering the *Lady Liberty*. Not even a lick of paint disguised the old and tired boat that had belonged to his parents, the previous owners of Sapphire Cay. He pressed his lips together thoughtfully. How long *had* it been? It felt like a lifetime. His parents had sold just over fifteen months ago, and he had been deployed to Afghanistan four months before the sale.

"Four years, more maybe," he said. Lowering his eyes, he returned to watching the ocean. The fresh October breeze whipped around him as the boat broke through the water's surface. Foam betrayed their path from Marsh Harbor and he looked back through his shades as they traveled parallel to the coast, circling the point as they headed for Sapphire Cay.

"Name's Scott by the way," the man said and grinned over his shoulder. He had no clear accent but that didn't really surprise Jamie. Another waif or stray adopted by the Cay, he figured. His parents had had a habit of taking in strangers, offering them a place to stay, and giving them employment.

Scott seemed friendly enough—dark hair, a deep tan, muscular, sexy, but totally *not* what Jamie needed. Scott met Jamie's eyes through his shades and flashed a confident smile—not his type at all. In a figure-hugging white A-shirt and low-hanging cargo shorts, Scott struck him as a player, a man who probably spent more time in front of a mirror than being an attentive, giving lover. Lover? Was that really where his mind was at? More likely, he just needed a release from the low ache in his chest and the memories that had him waking in a cold sweat and dry heaving in the toilet bowl. Closing his eyes, he savored the refreshing feel of the salty mist. He was judging a guy he didn't even know and it irritated him he could do it so quickly. That wasn't like him.

"So," he said. Conversation might help ease his mind. The man had been nothing but polite since they met on the quayside. "What do you do out here?"

Sapphire Cay had up to twenty staff at any one time he recalled—some permanent, some seasonal, and some on their own schedules. He had never come across the new owner, Dylan Gray, though he had heard good things. His parents loved the man and had been happy and relieved when he had decided to take on the island. They seemed to think Dylan was the perfect fit for what they had created during their thirty years out there.

"Captain of this fine vessel, excursions and tours, and

general help-where-help's-needed kind of guy," Scott said and flashed his teeth in a wide smile.

So Scott was someone who got stuck in and took to any role, not just the overconfident asshole Jamie had thought. He really needed to work on his people skills. Never the social butterfly, he felt even more inept than usual.

"Have you been here long? I don't remember you. Sorry if we've met," he said above the sound of the boat's engine.

"No. We haven't met," Scott assured him. "I came out here for the first time two years back with Dylan. We met in Thailand while traveling. He was heading out this way for a few months so I joined him. Luckily, your folks had work for me."

"And now?" Jamie asked. Dylan owned the island. There was no more moving on to the next place every month or two. "He's been running this place for a full year. He must miss it, the traveling."

"I guess a little. But he's settled and doing a damn good job." Scott raised his voice as the boat lurched forward, riding through a wave as it loudly hit the front of the boat.

"And you?"

Scott shrugged. "Let's just say Dylan's flexible, as is my contract. There's a job for as long as I want it." He pointed, directing Jamie's attention beyond the front of the boat. "There she is," he said. "She's something, right? I can see how Dylan fell in love with her so easily."

Jamie carefully got to his feet and stepped over his bag to stand beside Scott. He never thought seeing Sapphire

Cay would make him feel the way it did. Familiarity and memories flooded through him and almost knocked him off his feet. Maybe this hadn't been such a good idea. The Cay had been his home, a place of warmth and security. Schooled on the mainland, he always looked forward to rejoining his parents when the semester ended. His mom would always have the chef whip up a batch of his peanut butter caramel cookies. They would be sitting on the kitchen table when he and his sister had gotten home. What waited for him on the island now?

"Is Dominiq still there?" The chef had worked on the island since before he remembered. He was as constant as the tide and just as soothing. With an accent that dripped comfort and home, Dominiq was the epitome of relaxed, chilled, and taking it easy. Jamie was sure if he Googled any of those, he'd find an image of Dominiq smiling back at him. The man was a true Bahamian—dark skin, dark hair, the deepest brown eyes, and an easy smile. He never did figure out exactly how old the man was. For all the years Jamie had known him Dominiq had looked exactly the same, and only in his last few visits had Jamie noticed the whispers of gray creeping through his tight, black curls.

"Yeah," Scott said, bringing Jamie back to the present. "He's been baking all morning." Scott shrugged. "He's suddenly got this freaky cookie fetish going on. There were trays of the things cooling all over the kitchen."

Jamie couldn't help but smile. Things might not be so different after all.

"Must be strange coming back now that your parents have left. They're in Miami, right?"

"They are," he said as he took his seat.

His parents, now in their sixties, had talked about moving back to the mainland for years to be closer to family, especially their grandchildren. Jamie and his sister had their own lives, and though the island would always hold a special place in both their hearts, it just wasn't what they wanted to do. They weren't their parents.

Sue was a doctor with a husband and two kids. She was happy and settled. Jamie had joined the Marine Corps at twenty-two, straight from college. His squad had become his family for the next three years and he was proud to have served his President and his country. He knew his parents had asked Dylan to write in a proviso, entertaining the possibility of him returning to the island and doing some work out there. It must have seemed a strange request and yet, when Dylan agreed, Jamie kind of took to the idea of having somewhere to return to once his active tour ended. He just hadn't planned on it being so soon.

Instinctively, he rubbed at his chest and felt the raised line beneath his T-shirt. Seven months and the ghost of pain still clawed at his insides. Why wasn't it getting any easier? He stared at the growing outline of Sapphire Cay. Maybe on the island it finally would. He was here to get healthy, rediscover the man he used to be, and hopefully find a little peace. God love his mother, but he couldn't take a moment more of her fussing around him and everyone he knew treating him with kid gloves. He wasn't going to break. He wasn't that guy. Yes, something terrible had happened, but he hadn't been under any illusions when he enlisted. Bad stuff had happened to plenty of other people, and in some ways, he had been one of the lucky ones. Okay, so shrapnel from an IED ripping through his chest and shredding his right lung wasn't exactly a walk in the park, but he'd survived.

Light flashing in Jamie's eyes made him look up, and he was met by a curious expression from Scott. Damn, his mind had wandered again. He couldn't wait to get to the hotel and help with the repairs and renovations. He needed a distraction from his own mind.

Scott didn't voice the question that curled his lips into a thoughtful curve, but instead simply stated, "We won't be long now."

Nodding, Jamie returned to watching the ocean and the ripple of movement on the starboard side of the boat. A school of fish swam just beneath the surface, their scales shimmering in the sunlight and creating a kaleidoscope of color and shapes as they fed. He smiled to himself as he relaxed and watched the fish. It was good to be home in Sapphire Cay.

THE FAMILIAR FEEL OF SAND BENEATH THE SOLES OF HIS sneakers and the view of the hotel set back among the trees pushed from Jamie's mind any of the doubts he had about returning to the island. Spending time here, under the sun, would do him good. It was a chance to add some much-needed color to his skin and give him the opportunity to think. There were jobs for him in Miami if he wanted to stay local, engineering roles at the bottom of the ladder that would give him a chance to build on his degree and create a career away from the military. Spending time on

Sapphire Cay gave him the opportunity to think if Miami was what he wanted or whether it was time to move away.

"Dylan's put you in one of the staff cabins," Scott said as he dropped down from the small pier to join Jamie on the beach.

Jamie nodded and held out his hand to take his large bag from Scott.

Scott lifted the pack off his shoulder and passed it over to Jamie with a smile. "You're in the cabin at the end. Hutia."

The name of the cabin made Jamie smile. He remembered the year his parents refurbished the staff accommodations and spent several evenings selecting names for each of the updated buildings. Animal and plant species indigenous to the Bahamas had been agreed on. The Bahamian hutia was like a large rodent. Cute, Jamie figured, if you liked that kind of thing.

"You need me to show you?"

Shaking his head, Jamie said, "I can find it." He looked up at the hotel. It hardly seemed real, and as clichéd as it sounded, it really did feel like only yesterday that he was last standing here looking up at the building. Everything looked the same, and he inhaled, imagining the smell of his mom fixing breakfast.

"Housekeeping was in this morning, but if you find you need anything Agnes will be around until after lunch."

Agnes. He didn't remember an Agnes. "Thanks," he said, squinting against light reflecting off the white-painted building. "Are you hanging around?"

Scott shook his head. "I have to head back to Marsh Harbor for supplies. We have a wedding in six days, so lots to do." With a short wave, Scott hopped back up onto the pier. "Later," he said and flashed a bright smile before heading back to the boat.

With a sigh, Jamie stared up the beach. No point putting off introducing himself. Lifting his bag higher on his shoulder, he made his way up toward the hotel. The path was as he remembered, if not a little overgrown. The foliage was lush and green and overhung the edge of the roped-off route. Ridged wooden boards were half buried in sand and formed shallow steps for his trek upward.

As he reached the top of the short walk, he stopped and looked over the place he'd once called home. It now belonged to this Dylan and his partner. He just hoped they were taking good care of his parents' beloved past.

"Jamie?" The creak of the entrance door hinge drew Jamie's attention, and he was greeted by a man wearing an open white shirt and board shorts. "Jamie Durand?"

Jamie nodded and waited as the man made his way down the wooden steps to join him.

"Lucas," the man said and held out his hand. "Dylan's —" Lucas stopped and pressed his mouth in a line as he seemed to consider what to call himself.

"Boyfriend," Jamie said and shook Lucas's hand. He knew the couple were gay and together but kind of appreciated Lucas's attempt to not be utterly out. It was a trait he'd adopted as a Marine. *Don't be obvious.*

Lucas smiled. "Fiancé."

"Oh," Jamie said. "Congratulations." Lucas's eyes were a beautiful shade of hazel and amber and they seemed to shine in the sunlight.

"Thank you," Lucas said and ran a hand back through

his blond hair. He looked embarrassed as he turned away and glanced up at the hotel. "Dylan will be back in a half hour or so. He had some work to do down at the honeymoon cabin." Lucas turned back to Jamie and smiled. "He's actually been looking forward to you getting here. I'm kind of useless with a hammer so it's just him and Scott most of the time."

"Is there much that needs doing?"

Lucas gave a slow nod. "Bits and pieces. The usual before we open for guests."

Jamie remembered as a teenager following his father around the island from cabin to cabin, checking roofs and gutters and clearing fallen debris. One year, maybe eight years ago now, a tree had blown down and come crashing through the window of the hotel's dining room.

"We lay money aside for this and I'm sure among the three of you this place will be back to perfect in no time."

"Scott said you had a wedding. Six days, is it?"

"Yeah." Lucas rolled his eyes upward as he seemed to try to recall information about the booking. "The guests arrive on the twentieth, wedding on the twenty-first, two-week break, honeymoon, whatever, and they're gone by the fifth." He grinned. "And then we have about three weeks before the next party arrives."

"Another wedding?" Sapphire Cay accommodated for any occasion. Weddings, birthdays, straightforward vacations, there was even this one time some movie studio hired the island for a month. Extras in Speedos was definitely one of the times Jamie made an exception to his usual discretion. Shame none of the crew did. Though he hadn't realized it, his eyes had drifted down to settle on

Lucas's exposed tanned chest. Only when Lucas pulled his shirt closed and fastened the few buttons down the front of his stomach did Jamie quickly avert his eyes.

Lucas stepped past Jamie. "Yes. We have three before Christmas." He quickly looked Jamie up and down. "Do you have any other bags?"

Shaking his head, Jamie tightened his hold on the strap of his bag. "Just this."

"Okay," Lucas said. "But if you need anything, just ask."

There was something in Lucas's eyes and Jamie didn't want it to be the same as he had seen in so many people's eyes already. Pity. He didn't want anybody's sympathy or their *sorrys*. It was what it was and he needed to move on. He needed people to let him.

"Thanks," Jamie said.

"Sure. I'll take you to your cabin. See you settled in."

"You don't have to," Jamie said quickly. He was fine. He didn't need settling in.

Lucas smiled and started down the path leading around the hotel. "What kind of host would I be if I let you just wander off by yourself?" He held out his arms, indicating for Jamie to follow him. "And before you think it, I'm not trying to patronize you. I'm sure you know this place a hell of a lot better than me. I'd just like to make sure you have everything you need." He met Jamie's eyes and the *something* Jamie had seen was still there. To Jamie's relief it wasn't pity or sympathy or anything like that, it was more like anxiety. Lucas, it seemed, was nervous about Jamie being there.

"Okay," Jamie agreed. He figured Lucas just wanted

everything to go smoothly during his stay at Sapphire Cay. Jamie was, after all, the son of the previous owners and probably someone Lucas and Dylan wanted to impress. "Lead the way."

The short walk to the staff cabins was filled with idle chatter. Lucas seemed an okay guy. He was friendly and open and seemed to have a charm about him that had Jamie wondering what his fiancé, Dylan, must be like. The way he had heard it, it was Dylan who was the more carefree and laidback of the two, and if this was Lucas— happy, talkative, and easygoing—Dylan must be damn near horizontal most of the time.

"Here we go," Lucas said as he stopped outside the rodent-named cabin. The door was already unlocked, and Lucas entered the cabin first. "You have spare bedding and clean towels. Agnes will call in once a week to neaten things up. But if you need anything before that, she's around every morning and then again in the evenings." Lucas picked the room key up off the dresser. "I don't think much has changed. You're pretty much self-contained. But there's still the shared laundry area and we ask you don't use the main pool and things while we have guests. Otherwise, treat the island like your home. Well, like you used to, I guess, as it was your home." Lucas seemed to decide he was rambling and stopped. "I'll let you get unpacked." He handed Jamie the key and went to leave. Halting in the doorway, he turned back and looked at Jamie. "Come up to the hotel when you're done. Dominiq is making lunch." And with that, Lucas was gone.

Jamie let out a heavy sigh and looked around the open-plan living area. At the front of the cabin was the small kitchen consisting of an oven, refrigerator, sink, and two cupboards. There was a small couch, TV, and coffee table in the middle of the room, and then behind him a double bed, dresser, closet, and open door leading into the bathroom. Taking the few steps toward the bed, he dropped his bag to the floor and sat down on the end of the bed. Being here again after all this time felt strange, and the reason for his return unsettled him. He reached inside his T-shirt and pulled out the silver chain he wore around his neck. Sadly, he held the chain in front of him and stared at the tags threaded on the end. Light through the cabin window bounced off the metal tags as they swayed from side to side and Jamie caught them in his free hand. Squeezing his palm shut around the solid metal, he closed his eyes and reminded himself he was one of the lucky ones. He was home.

Chapter Two

"THE ORDER SAID PINK. NOT LILAC."

Edward stopped by Marylou-Beth's desk and couldn't believe what he was hearing. Was it possible that yet again the suppliers had sent over the wrong thing? *Jeez.* This wasn't the first, fifth, or even tenth time and his patience just about ran out when he took in the frown on his assistant's face. Gesturing for the phone, he waited until she said she was passing the phone over. Edward took the handset and counted back from five.

"I ask for twelve pink long-stemmed roses," he started. "You are not the biggest, best, or even closest supplier to me and when I order pink I expect pink. I don't run my business on near colors, and I don't want or need lilac. I expect a box of twelve pink roses to be delivered to my office by eleven am or I will take my business elsewhere. Consider this your last chance." He disconnected the call even as the supplier was blustering on about inclement weather and deliveries and transport and all the things that Edward shouldn't have to worry about.

"What if they don't send them?" Marylou-Beth said. She was chewing on a hangnail, which Edward found unsettling. Marylou-Beth didn't do that kind of thing. The action indicated something else was going on and he dreaded to think what other drama she was attempting to shield him from. Running a mental list through his head, he searched for potential problems. He had the Osborne wedding on Sapphire Cay and a civil ceremony at City Hall, but other than those there were no major crises that could cause his normally unflappable assistant to bite her perfectly manicured nails.

"What's wrong, babe?" he asked carefully.

"They sent the wrong color," Marylou-Beth wailed and then promptly burst into tears. *Hell.* He hated dealing with any woman crying, regardless of his huge affection for his assistant of two years. A transplant from her native Georgia after a failed romance, she was good at her job and kept him from being too anal about details. She had a good handle on his OCD tendencies and never ever thought it was okay to go through and amend anything in his diary. He clutched said diary harder. It never really left his side, was photocopied daily, and there was an electronic backup in three separate places. Nope. She never touched it, which was the perfect relationship between boss and assistant in his mind. He wasn't entirely sure what to do with the tears so he hovered uncertainly. Perhaps he should try and talk her down?

"It's fine, they're sending over the correct color—"

"What if they don't?"

Edward clutched his diary even closer. What the hell was going on? The only time he'd ever seen her this irrationally tearful was at the end of the last season of *America's Top Model* when the US lost out to Britain. Of course, Edward had been quietly proud but didn't have time to gloat as the waterworks kind of drowned out the end.

They'd watched it with sushi and authentic sake and she had just broken up with Tom; she'd sobbed this way for a good half hour. Which only meant… *Shit.*

"Did you break up with Tom again?" Edward asked carefully. They broke up at least every other month with some drama or another. And they said gay men were dramatic.

"He said—he—said—I was too tall—" She hiccupped the last. Edward's heart sank. So yes, she was a shade under six foot and Tom was only five nine, but they'd seemed so perfect for each other. He knew Tom, couldn't believe the man had actually said that the woman he called the love of his life was too tall.

"I'm sorry," Edward said. That was the right thing to say, and he wondered how long the drama would last. He was leaving for the Cay in two days and the office was hers. The last thing he needed was for prospective clients high on the need to get married to be greeted by a decidedly unattractive snotty nose and blotchy face. Then guilt swamped him. Hell, they'd been picking wedding themes yesterday and now Tom had broken Marylou-Beth's heart. Channeling his inner sensitivity, he scooted around her side of the desk and pulled her into a hug. Of course, that meant he was going to have deposits of shiny silver eye shadow on his black Forzieri button-down, but he could deal with it. He had a spare in the office closet.

Patting the top of her head with his free hand, he resolved to get Tom on the phone immediately to sort this out.

"Go out for a walk, sweetie," he said. "Get coffee, take ten, hell, take the rest of the day."

She pulled back and looked up at him; her violet eyes were watery and her lip trembled.

"I thought he loved me," she said.

"Of course he does. But don't you know, sweetie, all men are idiots."

"Except you. You're so sensitive and kind and sweet and you understand me."

Edward sighed inwardly but smiled outwardly. He was far from what she labeled sweet or kind. Sensitive yes, but he was of the belief that all men had the necessary skills to be sensitive—they just didn't use them. She buried her face against his shirt and sniffed dramatically.

"And you always smell so nice." Her voice had taken on a wistful tone, which was Edward's cue to back off.

"Thank you. Now go on, take a walk. A few minutes in the sunshine and you'll feel much better."

She scooped up her purse and headed to the door. "I'll never be all right again," she said dramatically, then left.

Edward immediately grabbed the handset and dialed Tom, who answered almost instantly.

"Edward, is Marylou-Beth okay?"

"What did you say to her?" Edward wasn't messing around with this; he had maybe ten minutes to sort this out.

"She had these heels on… all I said was that I liked them but that she made me feel a bit short." Edward couldn't believe how bewildered Tom sounded. Did he have no idea of how his fiancée felt about her height?

"Okay. Here is how you play this. Red roses—no chocolates since she's on a diet. Buy a tub of blueberry frozen yogurt instead, add a sparkler, and for goodness sake, spray some cologne before you come up. You have an hour."

"Got it. Roses. Yogurt. But cologne? Edward, you know I don't like that kind of thing—"

"Do it or lose Marylou-Beth forever," Edward said. Then he ended the call and shut himself in his office.

Changing his shirt was the first order of the day and he spent a good ten minutes making sure his shirt was tucked just so, his silk tie knotted perfectly, and his hair still frozen in its volumized style. Adjusting his black-framed Prada glasses, he peered at his reflection. They finished off the geek-chic look perfectly and he looked damn good, if he said so himself. As the owner and chief contact at Blush Pink Weddings, Edward McAllister had a public face and he loved it. The best designer clothes, hours at a salon for his thick, wavy dark hair, manicures, facials, everything he did made him the gay guy that potential brides loved and that potential grooms trusted with said brides. Blush Pink had grown year over year and he earned enough now to have Marylou-Beth as a permanent assistant and to run this office out of Coral Gables in one of the better areas of Miami.

The phone rang again and a cursory glance revealed Marylou-Beth wasn't at her desk. He answered on the third ring.

"Blush Pink, Edward speaking, how can we help you?"

"Edward. How's my wedding planner?"

"Fine," Edward said. "What's the problem?" He just

knew something was wrong from the fact Dylan had phoned and not Lucas.

"Small problem with next week." Dylan Gray's voice was low and calm. Hell, he could afford to be calm, it wasn't him that would be fixing last-minute adjustments in the wedding at Sapphire Cay. Edward liked Dylan a lot, but he wished it were Lucas he was talking to. Dylan had the grand ideas but it was Lucas who had the real business head. Dylan and Lucas were his biggest customers. Dylan even claimed Edward as 'my wedding planner'. It seemed that in the last few years, with the previous owners and now Dylan, he was spending more and more time on the Cay with weddings.

"What's up?"

"We have to do some structural work on the gazebo. Problem is that the electrical cable…"

Edward listened to the details and opened his diary to the page dedicated to the Osborne wedding. So. Probably no electricity to the gazebo. Which meant adjusting a few small details. Thoughtfully, he tapped a pen on the book as Dylan was explaining that they hoped to have it fixed but he couldn't promise anything.

Checking his calendar Edward mapped out the six days remaining to the wedding. He could work something that would be just as good.

"Edward? Are you still there?"

"It's fine," Edward said. "I can work around this. I'll take a look when I get there."

"Scott is booked to be at Marsh Harbor for you."

Edward raised his eyebrows. Edward used to love seeing Dylan waiting at the harbor, but since Dylan had

hooked up with Lucas—sorry, fallen in love with Lucas—
and was now off the menu, Scott would do as eye candy.
Scott may not be the man of Edward's dreams but he was
built like sin and was easy on the eyes. Shame he was a
player. Shame he wasn't Edward's type. Of course, you
could always look at the menu even if you don't plan to eat
from it. He chuckled at his thoughts. Scott would leap a
mile if he had any idea of the things Edward imagined
when he watched the man steer them from Marsh Harbor
to Sapphire Cay.

"I'll see you in two days, and meanwhile I'll email a
plan B for what I want. Or at least I'll get Lucas to do it."
Dylan added the last with a laugh and it made Edward
smile. Dylan and Lucas were so good for each other and
clearly in love. Seeing them together called to Edward's
romantic heart.

"See you in two days."

Edward closed his diary and leaned back in his chair.
The bride had wanted thousands of twinkling fairy lights
around the gazebo, which was now unlikely to happen.
Okay, so what else could he do? Images came to him of
the gazebo with the sea as the backdrop, and he
remembered the storm lanterns from previous weddings.
The glow of candles in the half dark would be stunning
and not nearly as intrusive as the brighter glow of the
strings of lights and if he had the candles reflecting
through colored glass…

Settled on what he needed to say to his picky bride, he
dialed her number. He was in the zone doing what he loved
best.

· · ·

SCOTT HELPED HIM OFF OF THE BOAT. IT WASN'T THAT HE couldn't manage but Edward wasn't going to argue with the help of a strong man. Brushing off the stray sand that decorated the ass of his suit pants, he cast a critical gaze around the landing area. This was the first point that the couple and their parties would see and it had to be perfect. Satisfied at the look of the old yet sturdy jetty and the wide-open expanse of perfect beach, he began the short trek up to the main hotel. The utter beauty that stood in front of him never failed to take his breath away. Low and wide, the hotel was wood and brick and solid in amongst trees.

Bypassing reception, he knew he had to see the gazebo and work out where everything was. He had photos but if there really was a problem with wiring that spread any farther then he needed to see it now and not later. He had a vague impression of what would work. The gazebo itself was a study in metal and wood and had weathered many a storm, and it would look stunning when he finished with it. He was in creation mode, the I-can-deal-with-anything frame of mind.

And then he rounded the corner and was faced with chaos.

Half the gazebo was missing. Literally gone. There was a hole in the middle where the wooden deck had been. A trench ran from the gazebo to the side of the hotel. It was utterly decimated.

"Four days," he blurted out. He caught movement out of the corner of his eye, a man walking backward, slightly doubled over and dragging an iron pillar that used to be part of the gazebo. Edward pushed away the instant appreciation of a fine, tight ass, powerful thighs covered in holey jeans, and the flex of muscles in strong arms. This wasn't some ten o'clock Coke break for him to ogle the laborers. This man was destroying his canvas. Edward couldn't form a sentence as panic knifed through him. He couldn't have the chaos in front of him now. He didn't have time.

"I'm sorry?" the man with the iron said. He turned to face Edward and Edward catalogued sweaty skin and a very young but serious face.

"Four days," Edward repeated. "What the bloody hell did you do?"

The man reached out a dirty, muddied hand with a smile on his face. "You must be the Brit. Dylan and Lucas warned me you'd be arriving this morning. I'm Jamie," he said. Edward looked at the extended hand and couldn't help the horror inside him from slashing angrily on his expression. What was *Jamie* doing here in the gazebo? Where *was* the gazebo?

"What have you done?" He gestured at the mess and was almost incoherent with shock. The last time he'd been faced with this was a garden party at his aunt's house when he had nothing more than paperclips to hold up banners. He'd been ten at the time and he was still traumatized by the stress of it. Four days to make something beautiful of this construction site? He could cover up… no… there was nothing… he couldn't hide this… no flower was big enough, no candlelight soft enough to cover the scar.

"You need to breathe," the other man was saying. He was patting Edward on the shoulder, those muddy worker's hands all over his Armani shirt, and Edward backed away. Disorder was in his head where he needed order.

"I *am* bloody breathing," he snapped. "Who did this here? Why is this happening in this wedding? Dylan never said…"

Jamie, the worker with the hands, was frowning and casting looks toward the hotel.

"I'll get Dylan—"

"Did they authorize this? Did anyone actually authorize what you are doing? Who the bloody hell do you think you are destroying the centerpiece of the whole wedding?"

"I work here," Jamie said. Like that was the whole defense for what he had done?

Edward snapped at the deliberately obscure reply. "Not for much longer you're not if you cause this much destruction."

Twisting hands in his hair, he stared helplessly at the mess for a few more seconds, and then giving Jamie-the-worker not a second glance, he stalked away to find Dylan.

It was only as he passed a wall mirror inside the door that he saw what he'd done. He'd literally pulled his hair to the point there was no style left in it at all. *Jesus.* He was already fighting sand and water and now he had to add dealing with stress to his haircare regime.

Breathe. Deep breath in. Out. In. Out. There had to be an alternative. Another way to make this wedding beautiful.

"Edward?" Lucas was suddenly there. He must have arrived while Edward was near hyperventilating. He was concerned and had that patented Lucas-look-of-worry on his face. Worker-man was hovering behind him and he also looked alarmed. "Jamie says you aren't well?"

"I'm fine," he snapped. "Well, I was until the kid here decided to play at building and ripped down the centerpiece of the entire wedding."

"Not a kid," Jamie said quickly.

"Do you realize this wedding is huge? Did you know the Osbornes went to five different planners before hiring me and this island? This could ruin my reputation. Why did no one tell me?"

"Calm down, Edward," Lucas encouraged. "We were working on the electricity but there was subsidence and the whole thing started to shift. It was dangerous." Lucas said all this with his hands held out, palms upward in a placating stance. "It only happened last night. Jamie, Dylan, and I have been up all night dealing with clearing what's left. I'm sorry." Lucas hesitated and Edward could see the exhaustion bracketing his friend's face. "I don't know what we are going to do," Lucas added.

Seeing Lucas worrying pushed Edward out of panic mode and into his normal take-charge default. Okay. First things first. Construction. He'd need dark-and-handsome-yet-hot-and-sweaty for that one.

"You," Edward said and pointed at Jamie. "Can it be rebuilt in three days?"

Jamie looked startled and then an expression crossed his face that Edward couldn't understand. A flash of fear or reluctance? It disappeared too quickly for Edward to get a real lock on it.

"I can do it," Jamie said. He crossed his arms over his chest and the movement revealed the impression of dog tags under his sleeveless T-shirt. *God.* Dog tags as a design accessory was so nineties. Edward shook the random thought from his head. *Focus.*

"You have two days to get me to a yes or no position. The Osborne party arrives in three days and I must have ideas of an alternative if the gazebo is a no-go." As Edward summarized his position Lucas was regarding him with a very odd expression on his face. The man had never really seen Edward in full-flight damage limitation before. Marylou-Beth said it was a sight to behold and scared the shit out of everyone in its path. Jamie disappeared out the back door without saying anything and Edward caught sight of that gorgeous ass again. Pity it belonged to the guy who was ruining his business.

Great.

There came his drama gene again.

Chapter Three

PARADISE SURROUNDED HIM ON EVERY SIDE, YET JAMIE found little comfort in its beauty. He focused on his breathing and the burn of exhaustion tightening across his chest as he ran down the beach. The wound to his chest may have healed on the outside but six hours of surgery had taken its toll. Despite all the breathing exercises and recovery time, he still felt a long way from okay and knew he would never really be one hundred percent ever again. The whole incident in Afghanistan had become shrouded in a thick haze. One minute he was on patrol, talking with the locals, and the next there was an explosion and muffled screams. All he remembered was the searing pain in his chest and the ringing in his ears.

The ocean lapping against the edge of the beach was his soundtrack as he continued his run. The low sound of waves rolling over one another reverberated in his chest and reluctantly, he slowed to a brisk walking pace before stopping completely. He suddenly became lightheaded and Jamie leaned forward and rested his hands on his knees to catch his breath. The dizziness began to pass as he took slow, deep breaths and he managed to suppress the bitter sting in the back of his throat.

Jamie's attention was drawn to sunlight dancing across the sand as it bounced off the hanging tags around his neck. Catching the swinging chain, Jamie pushed it inside the neck of his black wife beater and stood back up. With a sigh, he stared up toward the back of the hotel and the partially restored gazebo. He didn't have long to get it to a state where he could safely say he and Dylan would be finished in time for the Osborne wedding. The thing was a mess. The electricity still needed fixing and Scott needed to pick up some extra supports and… This wasn't quite the restful couple of months puttering around on the island he had been led to believe it would be.

Closing his eyes, Jamie took a few more deep breaths. A lot had changed in the last year. Things that used to come easily were now some of the hardest. He had always been fit and strong—hell, it came with the territory after all. Being in the military had been the best few years of his life. Yes, it was hard and there was pretty serious shit going on out there in the world, but with the friends he had made and places he had been, he wouldn't change a minute. Opening his eyes, he stared back up at the gazebo. He could fix it. He knew he could. If nothing else, he needed to prove to himself that things would get better—he'd be okay.

"Hey, kid."

Jamie looked along the beach and sighed as he saw Edward walking toward him. *Edward McAllister*. Jamie ran a hand back through his hair. The first time he had heard of the wedding planner had been through his mother a few years back. The way he remembered it, his mom spoke about Edward as if the sun literally shone out the man's ass. He had been told Edward was charming, funny, and 'totally now'. *Totally now?* Jamie had laughed so hard his sides had hurt at hearing those words roll off his father's tongue.

Even at seven in the morning, Edward managed to look perfect—skinny jeans, a burgundy shirt and tie, and a fitted waistcoat that hugged his slim waist. Despite first impressions that the man was a dick, Jamie had to admit Edward looked good. The front of Edward's hair was sculpted upward and Jamie found it hard not to think of the *Jimmy Neutron* cartoon he had watched as a child.

"So, the gazebo?" Edward said bluntly as he stopped in front of Jamie.

"Good morning to you too," Jamie said and folded his arms across his chest. Though unintentional, he felt the ripple of muscle flex in his arms and chest and smiled as he caught Edward eyeing his biceps from behind his tinted glasses.

"Is it?" Edward said, averting his eyes and looking out at the ocean. Tension radiated from him as he pressed his full lips into a pout.

Jamie felt a flash of guilt. He understood Edward's need for things to be perfect. "Look, me and Dylan—"

"Dylan and I," Edward corrected him.

Jamie raised an eyebrow. The fucking nerve. Maybe he should take the day off and see how Mr Prissy Pants felt about that. "Dylan and I," he said slowly and clearly, "will do our best with the gazebo. We're spending the day on it once Scott gets back."

Edward nudged his dark-framed glasses higher up his nose and looked at Jamie. What was he thinking?

"Fine," Edward simply said. He turned on his heel, starting up the beach to the hotel.

"Good talk," Jamie called after him and rolled his eyes up to the cloudless blue sky. The man was still a dick.

HALF AN HOUR LATER, JAMIE JOINED LUCAS, DYLAN, Edward, and Dominiq in the kitchen. Sliding onto a free stool, Jamie rested his elbows on the countertop and watched Dominiq pile a plate high with freshly made pancakes. That had been one thing he had truly missed in Afghanistan, real homemade meals. He wondered when Dominiq would notice that the cookies he'd made for Jamie's arrival had all gone.

"Morning," Dominiq said as he spun around and placed the plate in front of Jamie.

Jamie eyed the huge pile of food. "Morning," he answered and picked up his knife and fork.

"Scott's heading out after breakfast," Dylan said, hugging his mug of coffee. "He'll be gone for a few hours." Dylan lowered his drink. "So, I thought in the meantime you could help Edward."

"What?" Edward and Jamie said together.

Dylan laughed as he looked between the two men. "I would do it normally but there's an issue with the accounts that Lucas wants me to look at. We thought the two of you could start setting up." He glanced sideways at Lucas, who lowered his head and distracted himself with some papers he had been reading. "You always say you need more hands, Edward. This way you can make a start without having to wait for the rest of the staff to arrive."

Edward straightened his tie as he leaned over his bowl of cereal and curled his free hand around his diary. "I need petite and dainty hands, not muscles and sausage fingers."

Jamie looked at his hands. He had pretty normal-sized fingers, *thank you very much.* "I'm sitting right here," he said and looked at Edward. He got that the man was borderline OCD but seriously, did he have to be so rude? Even for a Brit, Edward was beyond sarcastic and everything that came out of the man's mouth sounded condescending. Jamie's gaze settled on Edward's lips and all he could think was how he'd like to shut the guy up.

"I don't suppose hanging fairy lights and napkin folding are on your CV?" Edward said as he turned to look smugly at Jamie. He pressed his lips in a curled line and in that moment, Jamie didn't know if he wanted to hit or kiss the man.

"Well, that's settled then," Dylan said, the legs of his stool scraping across the tiled floor as he slid back. "I'll see you both after lunch." He rested a hand on Lucas's shoulder, encouraging his fiancé to follow him.

Jamie sighed and looked around the kitchen. Where the hell had Dominiq sneaked off to? He stared down at his pancakes and then glanced at Edward, trying to decide what to do about the uncomfortable silence between them.

"You live in Miami?" he finally asked. He shifted in his seat, awaiting the expected snappy answer.

Edward pulled his diary toward him, running his finger

along the spine of the bulging journal. "Yes," he said while looking at Jamie over the frame of his glasses.

"My folks are in Miami." He poked at the pancakes with his fork. "You worked with them too, right?"

"Sorry?"

"Antoine and Jeanie Durand. My mom and dad? They used to own the island."

Edward raised an eyebrow and his eyes widened momentarily. Evidently, he had just put two and two together. Jamie wondered if he was going to follow that thread further. Clearly, he had something else on his mind. He screwed up his mouth as he looked Jamie thoughtfully up and down. "Do you have a clean shirt?"

A shirt? Jamie pulled at a loose thread at the hem of his wife beater. "Why?"

Sliding from his stool, Edward hugged his diary to his chest. "Because you smell bad," he said.

Jamie sniffed at his armpit. Maybe he should have grabbed a shower and a change of clothes after his run. He looked at Edward, who pulled a disgusted expression.

"Neanderthal," Edward quipped.

What was this guy's problem? Spinning on his stool, Jamie watched in surprise as Edward huffily threw back his head and stomped out of the kitchen. "Okay," Jamie said and turned back to his pancakes. He prodded at his syrup-soaked breakfast. Dropping his fork, he lifted the edge of his T-shirt and smelled the material. Shrugging, he picked up his fork again. Edward was just making a fuss over nothing. He didn't smell that bad.

Still, it wouldn't hurt to get a shower. His shoulders

ached and the thought of a hot shower followed by two hours of light-duty work made him smile. After forking down the rest of his breakfast, he jogged the short distance to his cabin and skidded to a halt in the bathroom. He locked the door, stripped, and started the shower. Catching sight of himself in the mirror as he waited for the heat, he took a second glance. Then chuckled. He didn't blame the stick-up-his-ass-Brit for the comments. The run, the physical work, not shaving, and not sleeping all served to make him look like a man on the edge. The scar on his chest was pink and sensitive to the touch as he ran a finger top to bottom. The reaction of the nerve endings never failed to remind him of how close he'd been to not actually making it back here to the Cay. The steam filled the bathroom, and soon enough the scar disappeared in the misted mirror. He wished it was as easy to hide it on his skin.

The shower was hot, the shampoo smelled of something vaguely herbal, and when he had washed and rinsed three times his hair squeaked clean and he concentrated on shaving. He'd gotten used to this. In the field a shave was a luxury and a mirror that stayed intact long enough rare. On the odd occasion he was in a hotel or a billet with showers, he would stand under the never-ending hot water and remove the stubble from his face with a safety razor by feel alone. By the time he stepped from the shower, stubble-free and smelling of shampoo, he felt that he would pass even Edward's critical eye and apparently acutely sensitive nose. He wrapped a towel around his waist and grabbed a clean T-shirt and cutoffs from the closet. Deodorant sprayed, he dressed and then checked his appearance briefly before running some gel through his short hair.

There. That really was as good as it got for a Marine with scars and a more or less constant ache in his joints and a predominant love of physical work. He looked okay. Neat. Edward seriously wouldn't be able to disapprove.

Chapter Four

EDWARD PULLED THE BOX DOWN FROM ON TOP OF ALL THE others and ran his fingers down the list of contents. Box twelve: Lights. Carefully, he placed it to one side. There was no way he wanted a repeat of last time when he'd dropped a box and cracked one of the tiny lights. Damn thing originally took out the whole string, but even after being bypassed so the rest of the string worked there was still the missing light. Throughout the entire bloody damn wedding all he could do was stare at the break in the string. Sometimes his OCD-level attention to detail even got on *his* nerves.

He pulled another box down, this one marked with the single word 'Candles' and then shuffled to swap it with the one marked 'Nets for Favors'. Dominiq had dropped off the selection of candies he had made for the favors so that was another job that needed doing this morning.

"Where do you want me then?"

Edward stiffened and straightened. The bad smelling, yet oddly attractive and sexy-arsed Neanderthal had arrived. God knows what he was going to give the man to do. Not only was the idiot ruining the gazebo, but he was more suited to outside grunt work. What the hell was the man going to do to thousands of delicate lights and napkins? Steeling himself, Edward pivoted on one foot and nearly fell over.

Well hello, sexy.

Seemed like Neanderthal scrubbed up fine. Gone were the thick dark stubble and the bird-nest hair, not to mention the sleeveless and dirty *Die Hard* wife beater. In its place, dark and sexy had on a clean white T-shirt with the words 'Sapphire Cay' in luminous pink emblazoned on the chest. Hell, not only was it clean but it clung to every single inch of the muscles that had been on display when Jamie had been working on the gazebo. How had Edward missed that this man was carved from granite? His gaze traveled down to Jamie's long, muscular legs encased in light-colored denim cutoffs followed by some pretty fantastic calves. There was an incredible coiled strength in Jamie and Edward had somehow missed it all. He looked back up again and his gaze met Jamie's.

There was a frown on the guy's stubble-free and frankly sexy square-jawed face.

"What?" Jamie said suspiciously. "I showered, I changed, what else did I need to do?"

Edward swallowed his tongue, making sure his mouth was shut, and then concentrated on willing away the threatening erection that was already making his slim-fit pants tight. Coughing to cover what was essentially him staring at the man-meat in his view, he turned back to the boxes.

"Nothing. Just, you know dog tags went out of fashion with Nick Carter and curtained hair. Though, lucky for you I believe Bieber and Gomez are trying to bring them back."

"Two tours in Afghanistan as a Marine and I think you'll find that they are less a fashion statement and more a badge of honor." Jamie said this calmly and quietly, and the words made Edward instantly turn back to face the young man.

"I apologize," he said quickly. He couldn't give anymore because Jamie had moved away from leaning on the doorjamb and was now standing with his feet slightly apart and his arms crossed over his chest. Why was he so stupid? He remembered Jamie's parents, on the one occasion that they had talked at length, saying something about a son in the Forces. Jamie's expression was impassive but there was a spark of temper in his eyes, temper which was soon banked to a look of acceptance.

"Apology accepted," Jamie finally replied. He didn't uncross his arms though. Silently, in this strange face-off, Edward pulled himself back to focus on the wedding and the job at hand. Running through the mental checklist in his head, he knew exactly what needed to be done first.

"So," he began, "first off we need to get these lights up."

Jamie nodded, and finally relaxing his stance, he held out a hand for one of the boxes. "Tell me where and how many and I'll hook them up for you in the corners."

"No!" Edward couldn't stop the horror in his voice. "Each light has to be placed very specifically. There will be no hooking or placing them in corners. I'll hold one end and you'll tack the strings like I tell you."

Jamie shrugged. "Whatever, let's just do this thing. Scott won't be long with the supports and I need to finish the gazebo."

"Don't do me any favors if you don't want to be here," Edward snapped.

Jamie sighed noisily. "I'm here, aren't I? Let's just get on with this."

"I don't want you doing this if your heart's not in it." Edward wasn't prepared to let this lie. He needed someone with passion for what they needed to do, not someone going through the motions.

"I'm only hanging fairy lights, not creating a work of art," Jamie said with another frown.

"They're not just fairy lights." Edward attempted patience. "And this *is* art."

Jamie peered into the box. "Looks like standard Christmas tree lights to me."

"No." Edward snapped the lid shut and held the box protectively to his chest. "These lights are beauty and ambience and when we drape the silk over them you won't see the corners of the room or the ceiling, it will be clouds of twinkling stars in a moonlit sky."

"Okay, okay," Jamie said. Then he snorted a laugh and Edward could feel his control slipping.

"Are you laughing at me?" Edward demanded. He'd had it done to him before. Hell, he was called too girlie or too romantic or too anything that didn't fit into people's idea of 'men'. He'd gone through bullying at school because he chose art and design over football, because he'd been different. But he'd worked damn hard to get where he was now and no sweat-stained laborer was going to be laughing at him, no matter who he was related to.

"No, not laughing, promise," Jamie said. But the man couldn't keep the smile off his face and Edward lost it just a little.

"Get out," he ordered.

"Don't be stupid," Jamie instantly replied. He was still smiling at first, but when Edward didn't recall the order Jamie finally seemed to realize Edward wasn't kidding.

"This is serious," Edward said. "So get out."

"I'm not leaving. I'm here to help, so let me help." Jamie took a step toward him, so close Edward could see curiously dark navy flecks in his sea-green eyes, and then he motioned for the box. Edward hugged it even closer. "Give me the box."

"I don't want or need your help," Edward said firmly. "You might think it's stupid for me to want this wedding to be perfect. You may think that a thousand fairy lights is not something special. But when the bride walks into this room I want to bring tears to her eyes at the absolute perfection she is walking into."

Edward inhaled quickly when he was suddenly aware he had said all of that on one single breath. Jamie was looking at him with a stunned expression. And there they were, staring at each other again in some kind of weird impasse. Jamie's expression went from amused to serious to resigned, then he nodded. He closed his eyes briefly and then opened them wide and there was a real apology in their depths.

"I apologize," he said simply. "I didn't mean to make

you think I wasn't going to do the best you needed me to. I get this is serious."

"You do?" Edward couldn't help the suspicious feeling he had curling inside him.

"Of course I do," Jamie offered. Like Edward would believe that; he wasn't going to fall so quickly for the apology in those gorgeous green eyes. "I'm used to orders, so you tell me where you want me and I'll get you up—get these up—on the wall—ceiling." Jamie ducked his head and exhaled noisily. "Just give me the damn lights."

Edward passed box one to Jamie, who took it with a delicate touch so at odds with the look of the man. He listened to each instruction and used the small step stool to place each string just so. He didn't complain when Edward asked him to move things; he didn't argue when Edward changed his mind.

"Can you hold the step?" Jamie asked. They only had two more strings to get up and it would mean stretching over the space created by an air conditioning unit. The stool didn't look all that safe as Jamie extended his reach. Edward moved closer, something he had avoided up until now for reasons he didn't even want to think about. Jamie had one hand flat on the wall, the other holding the string of lights, and he was stretched to the limit to hook the lights around the unit. Every single muscle strained and Edward pushed down the sudden and incredibly erotic image of Jamie stretched naked on a bed with his hands holding the headboard and his body arching up under Edward begging for...

"Hello? Earth to Edward. Can you hold the step? And grab my waist?" Jamie looked down at him and Edward snapped himself out of images of a sweaty, naked Jamie begging for him to…

"Edward!"

This time Jamie's tone forced through the erotic images and Edward took a step closer, within touching distance of the Marine. With one hand on the stool and the other holding on to Jamie's belt, he observed from below as the string of lights was pressed into place. As soon as they were done Jamie relaxed the stretch and stood more upright on the stool.

"You can let go now," Jamie said with a smile.

God. That smile. Those eyes. Edward's hand remained on Jamie's belt and he was inhaling the most amazing scent of tea tree and sandalwood and man. *Fuck. Inappropriate.*

"Sorry," Edward managed. Then he took a few steps back and picked up another box to hold in front of his erection. If Jamie knew what effect he was having on Edward there were two, no maybe three, possible outcomes. Jamie wasn't gay and would kill him for coming onto him. Jamie wasn't gay and would laugh at him like he'd laughed at the lights. Or Jamie was gay—or mildly bi-curious—and would get the wrong idea and then maybe either kill him or laugh at him anyway.

"Is that more lights?" Jamie asked. He attempted to take the box from Edward but he clung tightly and then backed away.

"No. Napkins," he said.

"We need to fold them? I've never done this. Will you show me?"

Edward nodded. He could show the Marine a lot of

things. Like the way he could curl his tongue around Jamie's dick and—fuck. *Head back in the game.*

"I need the bathroom. Take five," he said. Then without a backward glance he placed the box on the table, left Jamie on his own, and fled to the bathrooms.

Locking himself in a stall, Edward slumped onto the closed toilet lid and buried his face in his hands. He'd never, not in all his years of being openly gay, ever had it so hot for someone. And where the hell had that come from? Jamie was a Marine, rough, ready, all-action, heroic —a save-the-world type of guy. And Edward arranged weddings and used his own flamboyance as a selling point. Jamie, gay or not, would never be interested in him or anyone like him. Pressing the heel of his hand to his erection, he concentrated on the bloody thing just disappearing and resolved to get his head right.

When he got back out to Jamie the other man was deep in conversation with Lucas, who laughed at whatever Jamie was saying. Edward couldn't help it; he immediately thought they were laughing about him.

"Okay?" he said when he reached them. "What's the joke?"

"Nothing," Jamie said quickly.

"Share with the class," Edward insisted.

Jamie had the grace to look away from Edward, which only meant it had been him they had been laughing at. Then Jamie looked up and there was mischief in his eyes.

"Don't tell Dominiq but I ate the remaining cookies in a predawn raid. He's on the warpath, and even though he made them for me, I don't think he expected me to eat all twenty-four in the space of a couple of days. Do we have the napkins now?"

Edward was thrown at the change of conversation. All he could think was A) they weren't laughing at him and B) where the hell did someone with Jamie's physique put that amount of cookies?

"How's it going?" Lucas asked.

"We got the lights up in the reception room," Edward said. "There are napkins to fold, and that's all Jamie can help me with"—*unfortunately*—"until the gazebo is done."

"Well, I'm going back to the accounts, and Jamie, I won't tell Dominiq if you don't."

Jamie shook his head ruefully. "He knows it was me really."

Lucas left and Jamie turned his attention to the napkin box and smiled. He waggled his fingers in front of Edward's face. "Gonna train this Marine with the sausage fingers to fold them, then?" he asked.

Edward returned the smile briefly. He wanted to make a joke at this point but he really did need these napkins folded a certain way and he couldn't afford to lighten the conversation too much. Crossing to the table, he sat and opened the box, pulling out piles of scarlet cotton napkins. Jamie slid in opposite, and picking up the nearest piece of material, he pulled it toward him.

"What now?"

Edward demonstrated the Diamond napkin fold and repeated it twice. He showed Jamie how to get it to stay folded and then pulled an empty case over and gently placed the one he had done in the base.

"I thought this was a small wedding. How come we

need so many?" Jamie was looking at the remaining pile with something akin to horror on his face.

"Twenty in the wedding. I need eighty folded, one each for the rehearsal, one for the wedding breakfast, and at least one spare for each in case of problems. I also need to pull together the party favors with the sweets that Dominiq made. So can you do the napkins whilst I tie the favors?"

"No worries." Jamie began with the first one. At first he was gentle and careful and a little hesitant. Then hesitancy turned to confidence, and with military precision the napkins began to fill the new box. Edward couldn't watch him; he had party favors to wrap. But every so often he looked up to see a man who was so utterly focused on folding each piece of material the right way. There was even a small glimpse of tongue when Jamie worried his upper lip with his teeth as he worked. Edward couldn't help but wonder if Jamie would use the same intense concentration on a lover. Would he make love to Edward with that same single-mindedness verging on obsession to detail?

Edward shifted in his seat and concentrated on the tiny curls of ribbon he needed to create. Forcing aside all thoughts of sexy Marines who may or may not be gay, he lost himself in thought. Scott's arrival pulled him from his internal musings and he found himself saying bye to Jamie with a simple wave and pushed away all feelings of disappointment that his eye candy was going.

He'd live with the disillusionment of crushing on the straight guy or being completely and utterly not what some guy wanted in his bed.

Just like he normally did.

Chapter Five

"YOU GOT IT?" DYLAN ASKED FROM ABOVE JAMIE.

"Yeah," Jamie grunted as he leaned his weight into the ten-foot beam, holding the support vertical.

Shifting his feet, he braced himself for the lift as they raised it upward before slotting it into the bracket buried in the ground. The beam dropped a couple of feet, securing itself in the ground, and Jamie stepped back, wiping his hands on the ass of his cutoffs.

"That it?" he asked and eyed the six hefty supports edging the hexagonal gazebo. Two days to go and they were almost there.

Dylan jumped down from the stepladder and came to stand beside him. "I wish," he said and grinned as he leaned down and picked up a hammer. "I need to go through a couple of things with Lucas. You okay to carry on alone for a while? I've asked Scott to come and help us with the roof later."

Jamie eyed the half-completed gazebo. The decking

was done and the strong supports for the original roof were in place. Not Katrina nor Sandy nor Edward himself were going to shift this thing. He smiled to himself. Hurricane Edward, blowing across Sapphire Cay and whipping up a storm.

"Is it just the panels?" He was sure the gazebo was probably a little too open plan for Edward's taste and Jamie could already imagine the nets and strings of white fairy lights the wedding planner would have him wrapping around the structure.

"Yup," Dylan said and held the hammer in his direction.

Taking the hammer, he rotated his shoulder. He felt stiff but okay. "Then yeah. I'll carry on."

Dylan patted him on the shoulder. "I'll be back soon," he said and headed toward the hotel.

With a sigh, Jamie stared at the five panels leaning against one of the palm trees edging the open area the gazebo sat in. His gaze drifted from the panels to the view of the beach and the ocean. It was beautiful and kind of perfect and so very different to anything he had seen during his tour in Afghanistan. He watched the motion of the water for a while, lulled by the calm sound of waves and birds. As lovely as it was, if he was honest, he wouldn't trade the life he'd had over there—his friends, his job. It was a life that was just never meant to be he figured, and it was time to look to the future and decide what his next steps were going to be.

Closing his eyes, Jamie shook his head. Standing, staring at the ocean wasn't going to get him anywhere nor the gazebo finished. Resolving to deal with one thing at a time, he picked up the box of nails and collected the first of the panels. It shouldn't take him long to secure them in place. Quickly taking the steps, Jamie made his way across the raised platform. He looked over the already-laid boards for imperfections and found himself laughing as he thought about slipping into 'Edward mode' as he scanned every square inch of the decking beneath his feet.

A sudden twinge in his shoulder had him gritting his teeth, and instinctively he grabbed for his collarbone as his hand went numb. "Crap," he muttered as the hammer and box of nails fell to the floor. The nails hit the decking, rolling over and into the only gap in the structure.

Fucking typical. The missing board allowed Scott access for the final test and wiring of the electricity. "Great," Jamie muttered and got to his knees. The gazebo stood on a raised base, and Jamie leaned forward to look into the dark hole. The decking was raised a good couple of feet off the ground and Jamie stared hopelessly into the dim space. There was probably some more somewhere, but he couldn't just leave them under there, Edward might spot them with his super OCD spider senses.

"Plan B," he said with a snorted laugh.

Getting to his feet, he left the decking and crouched down beside the steps. Carefully, using the hammer, he pried the boards away from the structure until he had space to lean underneath.

"Where are you?" he said to himself and found the patch of light shining through the gap in the decking above him. Ducking his head, he leaned farther under the gazebo and reached out. "Gotcha." Wrapping his hand around the box of nails, he slowly backed up.

"What are you doing?"

Startled, Jamie lifted his head as he was tapped on the back. "Christ," he growled as he smacked his head hard on the wooden beam above him. He stopped and rubbed his head at his hairline. "Son of a bitch," he hissed as he held his head.

"Are you okay?" Edward asked and leaned down behind him.

Slowly, Jamie crawled backward, keeping his head down as he emerged from beneath the gazebo. "I'm fine," he grunted and sat back on his heels. He looked up at Edward. The man actually looked concerned.

Edward cleared his throat and shifted his weight at his hips. "Sorry. I didn't mean to startle you."

Rubbing at his head, Jamie winced. "No worries," he said and wiped his hand across his T-shirt.

"Oh." Edward leaned back. "You're bleeding."

The reddish-brown smear across his white T-shirt left Jamie feeling woozy. He had been shot at and almost blown up. A bump to the head was small in comparison, yet still it made him feel dizzy. He was weaker than he thought. "It's just a little blood," he reassured. Whom he was trying to convince was another matter. "Head wounds always look worse than they are." Edward had a less than convinced look on his face. "Honestly, it's fine." The last thing he wanted was the already paling Edward passing out on him.

Edward shook his head. "Don't be so stubborn." He

moved closer and inspected Jamie's forehead. "I'm sure you'll live. But we should maybe go get you cleaned up."

Jamie looked at Edward curiously. Why was he being so nice all of a sudden? Tilting his head, he looked into the deep brown of Edward's eyes. There was a warmth in them he had missed before. Maybe the man wasn't as far up his own ass as he had first thought. "Fine," Jamie conceded.

"I'm sure they must have some plasters, erm Band-Aids, or something at reception," Edward said with his hands.

"I have some in my room," Jamie said and reached out to Edward for some help to get to his feet. Edward simply looked at Jamie's hand, a frown creasing his brow, as he seemed reluctant to take hold of it.

Whatever. Jamie got onto his hands and knees and then pushed himself to his feet. Wiping his hands on his T-shirt, he then went to touch his head, but was surprised as Edward caught his wrist.

"Your hands are filthy," Edward said snappily and released Jamie's arm. Reaching in his jeans pocket, he pulled out a pack of tissues. "Here." He took a tissue and handed it to Jamie.

Jamie gave a crooked smile. "Thanks," he said and pressed it to his head. Pulling it away, he looked at the bright red stain. He should probably go see to it. "If Dylan or Scott comes by, tell 'em I'll be five minutes."

"I'm coming with you," Edward insisted.

Jamie quirked an eyebrow. "Why?"

"I'm not getting the blame when you pass out, swallow

your own tongue, and we find your bloated body in a couple of days' time." Edward sounded creepily serious.

"Wow," Jamie said. "That's real sweet of you."

Edward pursed his lips and shrugged. "I'm often told I care too much." He gave a wry smile and turned on his heel. "Let's go sort your head out. I have three hundred pieces of 3-D butterfly confetti to plump up."

The motion of Edward's hands as he spoke had Jamie smiling. "Okay," he agreed and held out a hand for Edward to lead the way. Pressing his mouth in a line, he watched Edward walk away. The man's skinny jeans hugged his figure and Jamie couldn't pull his attention away. He obviously had a concussion, he thought as his lips curled into a smile, and he followed Edward in the direction of the staff living quarters.

"YOU DON'T HAVE TO STAY," JAMIE SAID AS HE OPENED the first aid kit. "I'm not about to keel over." He picked up the bottle of antiseptic and a cotton ball. He looked at Edward in the mirror. The wedding planner looked uncomfortable as he hovered in the doorway of the bathroom.

Their eyes met in the mirror and Edward flashed him a tight smile. "It's fine," he said sharply, folding his arms and leaning against the doorframe. "Not like I have anything important to get on with." He briefly met Jamie's eyes in the mirror. "You are going to wash your hands first, right?"

Jamie snorted. Even when attempting to be nice, Edward still came across as a prissy dick. A little dirt never hurt anyone, least of all a man used to hunkering down in the desert bleeding from open wounds. Jamie lowered his head and gently wiped at his split skin. The shock of the antiseptic in the cut made him catch his breath as the stinging pain made his eye twitch. "Shit," he groaned and tentatively wiped again.

"Here," Edward said, stepping forward and taking the cotton ball from Jamie's hand. "Let me. Do you realize the amount of bacteria you have on your filthy workman's fingers?"

Jamie turned to face Edward and grimaced. He opened his mouth to give the guy the whole spiel about deserts and wounds but closed it when Edward shoved him unceremoniously onto the closed toilet seat. Stumbling back, his shoulder caught the edge of the vanity and he couldn't stop the grunt of pain at the connection, but he did manage to stop the accompanying curse that almost left his mouth. Sucking up the pain coursing through him, he concentrated on the breathing exercises he had perfected. By the time Edward had peered at the back of the bottle and worked out the quantities of antiseptic he needed, Jamie had his control back.

"You realize this stuff has all kinds of chemicals in it."

"No, Edward, I didn't."

"What? You don't read the label?" Edward tutted as he used the small lid that doubled as a cup to dispense the right amount. He then proceeded to smother Jamie's skin with antiseptic, and he was positioned such that Jamie got another look at Edward's face close up. The wedding planner must wet shave because his skin was baby smooth, and his scent was an intriguing mix of cologne and hair product.

"How long does it take to do that to your hair?" Jamie asked. He hoped focusing on Edward's hair and not his full lips or the shade of his eyes was a safe bet.

Edward narrowed his eyes. "You did not just start a conversation about my hair," he said, dabbing a little harder at the wound and making Jamie wince.

"Not so hard," Jamie said.

"Stop being a baby. I thought you were a soldier."

"Marine, not soldier. And I thought you were a wedding planner, not a sadist."

Edward shook his head and, with a final flourish, wiped away any remaining blood that had trickled down Jamie's face.

"There, you actually have a clean patch now," he murmured. Jamie ignored the pointed remark. A suited and booted butterfly like Edward should try rummaging around in dirt under a gazebo and see how long his Armani-whatever shirt stayed clean. What was it with this man and dirt anyway? Edward went to place the bottle high up on the vanity at the same time Jamie stood up, which was an accident just waiting to happen. Jamie knocked his arm, Edward tried to catch the resulting falling bottle, Jamie tried to avoid the contents and didn't quite manage it. Antiseptic splashed from the wide-open bottle onto Jamie's neck and left arm and all down his T-shirt.

"Bloody hell," Edward snapped. "What did you do that for?"

Jamie looked down at his T-shirt and then back up at Edward.

"Me?" he said.

"You knocked my arm."

"You put the bottle up there without its lid."

At an impasse, they stared at each other. It was Edward who backed down first. Gripping at the material of the T-shirt, he pulled it slightly.

"You need to get this off. You shouldn't get huge quantities on your skin." He tugged at the material again and Jamie yanked his hand off.

"I'll change it."

"If you put it in to soak now it won't ruin." Edward reached for the hem again and Jamie stepped back.

"I can deal with it."

Edward shrugged and then smiled cautiously. "But I want to help—"

"You've done enough," Jamie said firmly. "Thank you but I can take it from here."

The hesitant smile slipped from Edward's face as he turned on his heel and left the bathroom, pulling the door nearly closed behind him. As soon as he was out of sight Jamie slumped back against the sink. *Fuck.*

Not only was his dick hard in his pants at just the scent of Edward and how close he was standing, but now he was faced with the man getting right up in his space. As he breathed, all he could smell was antiseptic. It reminded him of his stay in hospital and he didn't like to recall any of that time. He put the plug in the sink and then tugged his T-shirt over his head. He'd rinse it, then leave it to dry in the sun. He didn't know why Edward was worried about the torn and stretched scrap of material. It wasn't long for this world anyway. He stopped the water, poked at the shirt, and willed away the erection that pressed against his shorts. *Jeez.* That infuriating, bossy, prissy Brit was getting under his skin like no one ever before.

Glancing up he caught sight of himself in the mirror, and taking in the sight of his stubble and the shadows under his eyes, he sighed. It didn't help when his gaze traveled down to see the scars running in jagged zigzags on his chest and the neat surgical scar disappearing beneath his arm. Gently he placed a finger on them and felt the raised edge of the dark pink marks. He wasn't deliberately hiding them but he didn't spend a lot of time staring at himself in the mirror either. He had gotten them fighting for his country after all. But what he hated was when people saw the freaking things and didn't know what to say. When they stared at the scars and struggled to find the right words.

"Jesus, those look bad," Edward exclaimed. He'd returned for some reason. Jamie glanced at him and saw a box of bandages in his hand. Edward was supposed to go away so that Jamie could get his erection calmed down. The damn man coming back in here wasn't going to help.

"What?" Jamie snapped. Edward had wide eyes and a concerned expression on his face. *Great, he's going for the I'm-so-sorry-you-were-hurt route*, Jamie thought. From Edward, he would prefer the reaction where he couldn't find words. That would be easier to handle.

Edward stepped closer and placed a hand flat on Jamie's arm that Jamie shrugged off immediately.

"I knew you were hurt," Edward said. "But that looks worse than I expected." Edward reached out again but this time his fingers grazed the same scar Jamie had just touched, which crossed next to his right nipple.

"Stop that," Jamie managed. He attempted to step back but there was no room between him and the sink full of water. He plastered on his most stern and aggravated expression but Edward wasn't even looking at his face. In fact, his gaze was following his fingers as he traced a path from one scar to another and then down the muscles of Jamie's chest to his navel. Edward looked up and Jamie couldn't help the slight move toward him. There was something in Edward's eyes that wasn't pity or disgust. More like lust. When Edward moved that small distance until only an inch separated them and there was nowhere else to move, Jamie swallowed the desire that spread from his dick out through his entire body.

"Jamie..." Edward said softly.

God, he wanted Edward. He wanted the smooth skin and Edward's hands on him and he wanted to kiss. He leaned in and the anticipation of the kiss was utterly consuming. What would it be like? Would Edward be fire underneath his icy control? Would he lead, or would he be happy to bend over and let—

"Guys!" Jamie jumped and Edward spun on his heel. Scott stood in the doorway looking at Jamie with concern on his face. "Dominiq said Edward was looking for Band Aids and that you got hurt. Is everything okay?"

Jamie grabbed his sopping wet T from the sink and squeezed it quickly before sliding past Edward and attempting to not touch him.

"I'm fine," he said shortly. Then before either Scott or Edward could say anything, he encouraged Scott to move to one side and escaped out into the heat of the midday sun.

Hiding behind the gazebo was one way to avoid Edward and he stayed there until he was erection free and his T-shirt had more or less dried. Jamie had been in short relationships before, but never had an exchange of silence as charged with sexual tension as that one.

He was lost.

Chapter Six

"What was that all about?" Scott asked. His voice held as much confusion as Edward felt at that moment. They'd almost kissed. He could swear that he and Jamie were so close to kissing. He wanted to kiss Jamie. What would he taste like? What kind of touch would he have? Would he be hard and pushy or melt into Edward? Bloody hell, he was so hard. This was getting to be a habit whenever he was within a foot of the Marine. Being faced with Jamie's chest, all muscled planes and a V that ended at his navel, was overwhelming. He'd even seen the hint of Jamie's treasure trail pointing down to his dick, which Edward couldn't fail to notice was just as hard as his was.

"Earth to Ed," Scott said. He snapped his fingers in front of Edward's face.

"Sorry. What's wrong?" Edward said. He wasn't really following what Scott had asked him, lost in the swirl of emotions that refused to settle inside him.

"Was Jamie okay?"

"Jamie?"

"You know…" Scott indicated the box in Edward's hand. "The Band-Aids. Blood. Enough antiseptic to sterilize the entire island."

"Oh. That." Edward touched his head in the position where the blood had been on Jamie. "He just bumped his head."

"We should get him to the mainland," Scott said quickly. "What if he has a concussion?"

"He's fine." Edward forced himself out of his confusion and pulled back his shoulders. He could do calm and controlled. He was good at that. "Are you going out to help him?"

"What crawled up your ass and died?" Scott said quickly.

Edward sighed inwardly. He couldn't help it that, on top of his usual desire to see the wedding go well, he had this weird overwhelming attraction to Jamie.

"Nothing," Edward replied.

"Well then," Scott muttered. He left the same way Jamie had gone and Edward was left standing in the hallway with a box of plasters in his hand and his mind all over the place. This wasn't good. He needed to get some control here and get his head back in the game. Jamie was not his type. Jamie was so far the opposite of his type.

Huffing, he turned and left in the other direction to Scott, just because he could. He needed to check on the electricity at the gazebo, it was next on his list. That was what he had been going to look at when he'd surprised Jamie and made him hit his head. Coming to the gazebo from the front, he was pleased to see it was standing very much together, and he narrowed his eyes trying to imagine the wood and metal softened by the lights and the growing dusk. He couldn't see either man at first but then he saw Scott shuffling backward with more wood and Jamie taking the other end. Instantly, blood rushed to his dick and desire for that kiss swept over him.

Not. Again.

Why couldn't he get hard over Scott? Scott was easy, fun, normal, not dark and taciturn with a history. And young. When he'd looked up from examining Jamie's chest and stomach and their utter perfection he'd caught a vulnerability in Jamie's expression that wound its way around his heart. The Marine had looked impossibly young at that point. Not that twenty-seven was much older than the twenty-five-year-old Marine. For a while he watched and made mental notes about things that needed doing, and then reluctantly he moved back inside to get to his diary and tick off more items on his list.

THE GAZEBO LOOKED GOOD. OKAY IT WAS DARK BUT THE wiring was fixed and tomorrow he could get the lights on it. The structure was sound. He'd checked the wooden flooring and tested the steps, and really there was nothing else that could be done. This was one of his favorite places on the island, and he'd seen five couples married under the beautiful metal and wood shelter. Here, with two days to the wedding, he could relax and stop worrying simply because he wasn't able to do anything else tonight. Leaning back against the rounded metalwork, he tipped his head back and looked beyond the side up into the night sky. If only he could stop the unsettling thoughts he was having about Jamie then he might be able to truly relax.

"We're landscaping tomorrow."

Edward accepted the inevitability that Jamie would follow him here. They'd played gaze tag at dinner. Jamie would look at him and he would look away; he would look at Jamie and Jamie would refuse to meet his eyes. When he'd made his excuses and said he needed to check on the gazebo, Jamie hadn't immediately stood up as well. But there were things between them, unspoken questions that needed to be answered.

"Good," Edward answered.

"Scott is talking about hefting some stones and pots around to cover some of the scarring from the cabling. I'm leaving it to him. Did you know he has a degree in horticulture?"

Edward crossed his arms over his chest. So they were playing the game of avoiding the elephant in the corner. He was a Brit; he could do that in his sleep.

"No, I didn't know that about Scott."

"Yeah. He's good at that detail stuff." Jamie took the three shallow steps up to the main area and leaned on the banister opposite Edward. "I'm more the hauling type," he added. "Grunt work."

"Don't put yourself down," Edward said. "You did the carpentry on the flooring and the metalwork. You're clearly skilled with your hands."

Silence.

Jamie finally broke the silence with a laugh. Then Edward smiled at what he just said. He'd had heated thoughts about what Jamie could do with his hands.

"So. Weddings then," Jamie offered as a starter for conversation.

"Weddings," Edward repeated. When Jamie said nothing else Edward assumed he was meant to keep the conversation going. "Someone I knew got married when we'd both just turned nineteen. I knew her in school, and as her 'gay best friend' it fell to me to make the wedding good on a budget of five dollars and a handful of change. Been doing it ever since."

"Bet the weddings here cost more than five dollars," Jamie observed wryly.

"Just a bit."

"So. The bathroom thing." Jamie sounded confident and very focused on what he wanted to talk about suddenly.

Wow. Talk about getting the elephant by the trunk and dragging it out of the corner.

"Your head." Edward thought deliberately misunderstanding might buy him some more time until he could get a hold on his emotions and thoughts.

"Not that. The kiss."

"We didn't kiss." *I would have remembered kissing you.*

"We nearly kissed," Jamie insisted.

"I'll give you that."

"We need to settle this one way or another. You don't like me. I'm rough, dirty, and not your type." Jamie counted the items off on his fingers. Evidently, he had been giving this a lot of thought. Edward frowned.

"And you think that I am uptight, dress too well, and do a woman's job."

"I never said any of that," Jamie said. He moved away from the banister and stood tall.

"Well, I never said that you weren't my type."

Jamie huffed. "So you're saying that you can shut your eyes and pretend I'm all silk and linen when actually I'm basically navy-issue cotton."

"Who said I wanted silk and linen, and what the bloody hell does that even mean?" Edward took a step away from his side of the gazebo.

"You said I had sausage fingers. You said I needed to wash my hands."

"And you looked so good when you'd showered and shaved," Edward protested.

"That's not me. Not all the time."

"I don't want it to be all the time." He could hear their voices getting louder and more heated. Was this an argument? Edward didn't normally argue. Typically, his Britishness allowed him to get away with a lot when he dealt with frustrating people. He was allowed to be icy and calm.

"What are we even talking about?" Edward finally said. He realized they had both stepped closer until only a couple of feet separated them. In the dim glow cast by the lighting from the main house he could see the stubborn expression on Jamie's face.

"We're discussing what it is that you want," Jamie said bluntly.

"Then what is it that *you* want?" Edward said quickly. He was damn well getting turned on by this barely held in aggression he was feeling. He was really looking at Jamie and wanted him more than his next breath.

"You," Jamie whispered harshly.

Time seemed to stop. Edward heard the sounds from inside the house, the noise of the ocean against the shoreline, and suddenly everything snapped into place with a dazzling clarity. Who moved first, he couldn't tell, but when they met in the middle the clash of their lips and hands was explosive. Jamie was everything Edward needed at that moment—strong and kissing him with a ferocity of need that matched Edward's.

They battled for control and then Jamie pulled back with a dazed expression in his face. His lips were wet and he had a firm grip on Edward's biceps.

"Let me," he pleaded. Then he slid his hands down to Edward's and held them momentarily.

"Let you?" Understanding the plea was difficult, which he blamed on the incendiary kissing.

Releasing his hold, Jamie cupped Edward's face and stared intently at him. Then he leaned the rest of the way and kissed him. This time it was Jamie controlling the kiss, and Edward melted into the embrace and the sensations. He held on to Jamie and rested his hands on the belt of his cut-offs momentarily before sliding down to explore the tight behind he had been admiring since they first met.

He never wanted this to end.

It had to end.

Jamie tilted his head to deepen the kiss and Edward couldn't deny himself the passion if he tried. Jamie was hard against him, and the kissing... God... the kissing. When they parted again Jamie stepped back and held out a hand.

"Let's go somewhere and kiss some more," Jamie said.

There was a question in there somewhere. What was Edward agreeing to by saying yes? More kisses? Sex? An affair? A relationship? He had no idea what the end game was. Finally, there was only one decision he could make.

He took Jamie's hand in his. "Okay."

LEADING EDWARD BY THE HAND, JAMIE HEADED DOWN toward the beach. He tightened his hold on Edward as they ducked to avoid a low hanging palm, and a mixture of desire and fear sparked in his chest as Edward's body brushed against his.

What did Edward expect from him? And what was it he wanted for himself? Kissing was good. Kissing was always good. Lips on his, tongues tasting, and hands exploring. What more could anyone want?

A hell of a lot more. He hadn't had sex in over a year, with going to Afghanistan and then being injured. He thought back to the bathroom. Edward hadn't been disgusted or shown him any pity when he had seen the scars. In some ways it was refreshing and it made Jamie appreciate the fussy wedding planner and his quirky habits just that little bit more than he already had. Glancing over his shoulder, he looked at Edward and smiled to himself. In the low evening light, Edward looked as handsome as always and the idea of going beyond kissing had heat rushing to the head of Jamie's dick.

"Where are we going?" There was a hint of annoyance in Edward's voice as they made their way along the overgrown path, but Jamie chose to ignore it, turned around, and pulled Edward close.

They stood together beneath the shade of the trees, looking into each other's eyes. Their breathing matched the rhythmic pull of the ocean. The sound of waves against the shore, just beyond the edge of the trees, and the beautiful glow from the setting sun gave the moment between them a sense of magic.

Reaching out, Jamie cupped Edward's face and stroked gentle lines over his perfect cheekbones. There was a pristine beauty about the man, an effeminate charm. He hadn't had anyone special in his life in what seemed like forever, and despite Edward driving him to despair with his British snippiness, he was finding there was more to the straight-laced wedding planner than met the eye. He smiled as Edward pouted and looked expectantly up at him.

Testing the connection, Jamie moved forward and ghosted the lightest of kisses over Edward's mouth. The feel of Edward's breath on his lips and the scent of mint had Jamie keen to continue. Teasingly at first, he kissed Edward periodically, leaning his body into Edward's as he moved him back against a tree. He cupped Edward's face, reassured as Edward wrapped his hands around the back of his neck in return, and held him close. Encouraged, Jamie deepened the kiss and pressed his body firmly to Edward's. The feel of Edward warm and undeniably hard against him had Jamie's stomach doing back flips, and as Edward let out a delicious groan Jamie knew the man had felt his erection as well.

Time lost all meaning and eventually, as the light

began to fade, Jamie broke the kiss. Edward licked his plump lips and looked up at him through his lashes. There was no denying it, Edward was a beautiful man.

"Come on," Jamie said and took Edward by the hand again, leading him toward the beach.

Neither man said anything else as they made their way from between the trees and out onto the sand. The sun was almost gone, illuminating the ocean with a peach and purple glow as it disappeared behind the horizon.

"You know what I missed," Jamie said as he held Edward's hand, "when I was away in Afghanistan?" He looked at Edward, who simply shook his head. Gently, he squeezed Edward's hand and raised it slightly. "This."

He had always put his job first, always taken it seriously, but with that, to a certain degree, came the denial of who he really was and who he loved. He was a gay man living in a perceived-straight world.

"Holding my hand?" Edward said curiously.

"Yes. Well, anyone's hand." He laughed. "Just being myself. No prejudice." Still holding Edward's hand, he walked down the beach toward the water. The tide was on its way out and he stopped at the edge of the dry sand. Releasing Edward, he sat down, pulling up his legs and crossing his arms on his knees. When Edward didn't join him, he lifted his head and looked up at the wedding planner, who shifted uncomfortably beside him.

"You okay?" Jamie asked. "I don't expect anything."

Edward shook his head. "No, it's not that." He shuffled his feet and ran his hands over the ass of his jeans. "Sand," he said as an explanation.

Jamie quirked an eyebrow and brushed his fingers over the fine, grainy surface. "It's dry," he assured Edward.

"It's messy," Edward added. "Do you know how hard it is to get it out of your clothes? Like really out? All of it?" He wore a serious expression as he eyed the ground.

Jamie looked at the water as he tried not to laugh. Two ideas came to mind. One involved grabbing Edward by the wrists and dragging him down onto the sand, which would probably kill any chance of more kissing, or there was option two.

"Here," Jamie said and pulled off his T-shirt. "It's clean." He spread the material out over the sand and indicated for Edward to sit down beside him. He waited, smiling, as with a huff, Edward sat down on the T-shirt. "Ish," he added, and this time couldn't help but laugh as Edward glared at him.

Seeming to make himself comfortable, Edward rested his heels in the sand and leaned his elbows on top of his knees. They sat in silence for a few moments until finally, Edward spoke.

"So, what happened?" he asked and met Jamie's eyes. His gaze drifted to Jamie's flawed chest and the scarred marks.

Jamie breathed in deeply. He hadn't really talked to anyone about it. Yes, he had been sent to a therapist to help him deal with what happened, but he wasn't good at talking about his feelings. He knew his parents were worried, but they shouldn't be. He was doing okay and as soon as he felt up to it, he would do what everyone seemed desperate for him to do—move on and get on with his life.

"Would you believe me if I said I don't remember?"

He lowered his head and looked at the sand between his feet.

"Maybe, if you sounded a tad more convincing." Edward smiled as Jamie gave him a sideways glance.

Sniffing a laugh, Jamie ran a hand back through his hair. "I don't remember everything, but I remember this loud noise, an explosion, and then screaming and blood." He looked at Edward. "My blood."

"You're very brave," Edward said. "I could never be that brave."

"It takes all sorts." Jamie rested his arm across his chest. He hadn't realized it before, but with the loss of the sun and being so close to the water his skin was cool to the touch.

Edward shrugged. "I don't think setting tables and stringing fairy lights is really up there with fighting for your country."

Jamie grinned. "Oh I don't know. Some of those brides can be pretty scary, right?"

"True," Edward said with a laugh. "There was this one woman a couple of years ago. Your mum would remember her. She'd had a fake tan and looked like an Oompa-Loompa. It was funny until she threw a hissy fit, and somewhere along the way it all became my fault and I was ruining her special day."

"What did you do?" He couldn't imagine Edward shying away from the confrontation.

"Gave as good as I got, obviously."

"I can imagine," Jamie said and slowly ran his hands up and down his arms. He hoped Edward appreciated his gentlemanly consideration for the well-being of his pants.

He sighed as he stared back at the water and his thoughts drifted to his last mission.

"I thought I was going to die." He closed his eyes as Edward gently touched his arm. Edward's hand was warm and comforting.

"You didn't." Edward shuffled closer. "And for that, I'm glad."

Jamie opened his eyes as Edward pressed his warm, solid body to his side. He looked at Edward and tilted his head slightly. The man looked at him with such desire and warmth. Twisting around, he slid his hand around Edward's neck and pulled him forward into a kiss. This was what he needed—a warm body and an emotional connection. He needed to feel alive and that life was still there to be lived. Closing his eyes, he held Edward close and kissed him passionately. This was as good a place to start as any.

Chapter Seven

EDWARD'S ROOM WAS AS IMPECCABLE AS JAMIE HAD imagined. The brilliant white bed sheets were neat and pressed, personal items had their individual and regimented place, and the whole room smelled as exquisite as the man himself.

"I could have used you during inspections in training," Jamie said as he stepped inside and pushed the door closed behind him. He looked down at his feet and the patch of sand he had tracked in. Carefully, he kicked off his shoes and pushed them up against the door.

"Drink?" Edward asked as he got two bottles of mineral water from the refrigerator. He held the water out to Jamie.

Brushing his hands on his pants, Jamie stepped farther into Edward's space. He felt like a kid again when he used to visit his grandma in Homestead. She was constantly following him and his sister around, eagle-eyed and reminding them to take off their shoes and not to touch the walls.

"Thanks." He took the bottle and licked his lower lip as Edward's fingers brushed the back of his hand. Taking a drink from the bottle, he looked around the room. "Who's that?" he asked as his sight settled on an expensive-looking silver frame and the picture inside it. There was Edward, a few years younger than he was now, with his arm around another man's shoulders.

"That's Andrew. My brother."

"Where's he?" Jamie asked as he continued to look around the room.

Edward slipped past Jamie and sat on the end of the bed. "Back in England. He lives with my parents in a quaint little seaside town in Devon."

"Do you go home often?" He used to love to come home after months away. It was only when he was injured and living with them again that he suddenly felt trapped and overwhelmed.

"This is my home. Well, Miami anyway. We moved out here when I was eighteen and Andrew thirteen, but it wasn't what they thought and they headed home after three years."

"And you stayed?"

Edward nodded. "I was twenty-one. I'd been to college and made friends, had a job lined up and a plan for the future. Seemed silly to give up on that."

Jamie sat on the bed beside Edward and stared at the wall opposite. "Now, that sounds brave."

"Maybe," Edward said and drank from his bottle. "I've been lucky, I guess. I mean, I'm twenty-seven and run my own company. Not everyone gets that kind of chance." He pursed his lips as he looked at Jamie thoughtfully. "So, what are your plans? You can't want to hang around here forever."

His plans? Did he really need a plan? "I don't know. It's one possibility."

"And the other?"

Jamie rubbed his brow. He'd toyed with the idea of using his degree and having a career. He'd been out there and doing for the last three years though. It was hard to imagine stepping back and starting again from the bottom up.

"There must be something you're interested in," Edward pressed.

"Engineering design, like for buildings and landscaping." He looked at Edward, embarrassed. "I know, me and my sausage fingers should probably stick to shoveling dirt and sawing wood, right?"

"Not at all," Edward said encouragingly. "Look at what you did with the gazebo, and your light-hanging skills are pretty impressive." He smiled and nudged his shoulder against Jamie's. It was nice to see the relaxed, lighter side of Edward.

Picking at the label around his bottle, Jamie shrugged. It was just an idea, something more than clearing gutters or swinging a hammer here on Sapphire Cay. Besides, he couldn't hide out on the island forever, real life had a habit of sneaking up on you.

"Besides…" Edward took the bottle from Jamie's hand and placed it on the floor with his. "Now I've seen them close up—" He lifted Jamie's hand and pressed their palms together before threading his fingers between Jamie's. "—I think you have nice hands." He held onto Jamie's hand and smiled, leaning forward to kiss him. "Very, very nice hands," he whispered against Jamie's mouth and then kissed him again.

Jamie pulled his hand from Edward's and laced his fingers through the back of Edward's hair. He'd get chastised for that later he was sure, but right now he nor Edward cared about the disheveling of perfect hair or the dry sand falling from Jamie's clothes and skin.

Getting to his feet, Jamie pulled his T-shirt off and quickly returned to kissing Edward, nudging the man higher up the bed as he straddled his thighs and leaned down, capturing his mouth over and over again. Distracting Edward with kisses, Jamie began to undress him, pulling at the buttons on his shirt as he desperately sought for access to Edward's skin. And then—finally—he was in and pulling Edward's clothes back and off his shoulders. Perfect was the only word to describe Edward. Slim and yet perfectly defined, Edward's body was aglow with an even tan and Jamie leaned forward, licking a line from navel to neck in his appreciation. Attentively, he circled each of Edward's dark nipples with his tongue, smiling as they each rose to a hard nub accompanied by a sensual shiver passing through Edward's body.

"Okay," Jamie said and placed a kiss to each nipple before crawling farther up Edward's body. For a moment, he held himself over Edward and looked down at the man beneath him. Gently, he slid Edward's glasses from his face and placed them on the other side of the bed. He tilted his head slightly as he looked over Edward's features. It was strange to see the man without his glasses, but he was just as perfect with or without them. Jamie leaned down and kissed Edward's soft, full lips. Tenderly, he held Edward's face, curling his fingers against his jaw as he melted into the man's arms.

Fuck, he wanted this man. He wanted to have the guy naked beneath him, wanting him, needing him. Not breaking the kiss, he moved one hand downward between them, lifting his hips as he fingered the fly to Edward's tight jeans. He pressed his hand to the hard bulge in the front of Edward's pants and smiled into the kiss as Edward gave a low moan. God, that sound made him harder than he thought possible. Fumbling with Edward's fly, Jamie finally succeeded in finding his way inside the man's jeans and then his underwear. Edward was so hard and so warm and all Jamie could do was wrap his hand around the head of Edward's dick and then begin a slow movement along his length.

Edward ground his body upward, pressing his erection farther and firmer into Jamie's hold. His hands came up and around Jamie's neck, holding him tightly as they continued to kiss. Jamie responded with an openmouthed kiss, sliding his tongue inside to battle Edward's for dominance. As their tongues danced together, Jamie increased the thrust of his hand, bringing Edward to the edge of something amazing. Edward tightened his hands on Jamie's back, spread his legs, and lifted his hips. Fuck, the image Jamie had in his head excited him and he swore it wouldn't take much more than a touch from Edward to make him a whimpering mess of sex and desire. God, he was so damn horny.

Shifting his weight, he straddled Edward's thigh and pressed his own erection against the man's leg. The friction had him groaning against Edward's mouth and the two men rocked and fucked against each other until a few unbearable and desperate minutes had them climaxing, Edward first and Jamie following. They lay together in an exhausted heap until Jamie reluctantly pulled his hand free.

"Pins and needles," he groaned, kissing Edward as he awkwardly leaned back on to his knees. Edward lay flushed beneath him, heat marking his chest and neck in pink patches. Scrambling backward, Jamie managed to get to his feet and adjusted himself in his pants. Well, this was all kinds of sticky and embarrassing and he quickly turned on his heel for the bathroom.

Closing the door behind him, he washed his hands and cleaned himself the best he could. He met his eyes in the mirror and brushed his dark bangs back from his forehead. Flushing the toilet, he left the bathroom with a washcloth and smiled as he found Edward still lying on the bed.

"You okay?" he asked. He passed the cloth to Edward and wiped his wet hands on the back of his cut-offs.

Edward ignored the cloth, blew out a breath, and stared up at the ceiling. "Yeah," he finally said and smiled as he looked at Jamie. "I'm great."

"We made a mess," Jamie pointed out helpfully.

"I'm too boneless to worry," Edward said. He hadn't made a move to wipe himself down and Jamie stepped forward and took the cloth back. In smooth, even sweeps he had Edward clean, and he followed each wipe with a kiss to smooth skin.

"How long does the boneless feeling of yours last before you freak out and want to change the sheets?"

"Three point two minutes," Edward deadpanned. Jamie chuckled and threw the cloth in the direction of the small laundry basket. Silently cheering himself when it fell directly in, he snuggled back under the sheets up against Edward. Didn't matter if Edward wasn't a cuddler, Jamie was going to take cuddling wherever he could get it. Almost three years in the Marines didn't lead to many occasions where post-sex snuggling was going to happen.

When Edward turned in his arms and arranged himself with one leg hooked over Jamie's and his left arm sprawled over Jamie's chest, it was perfect, a nice memory to keep for another day when he was back on his own.

Edward pressed a kiss to his shoulder and then trailed warm touches of his lips from Jamie's shoulder to the juncture of neck and chin. Jamie only needed to turn his head and he could capture Edward's lips for some more kissing. He only hesitated for a split second before he stole his first kiss, which Edward enthusiastically returned.

"I could do that all day, soldier," Edward said.

"Marine," Jaime corrected on a laugh.

"You'll have to explain the difference." Edward smirked. "With diagrams."

Jaime couldn't help the smile that curved his lips. This Edward, the one with the floppy, unstyled hair, ruined by Jamie's own hands, and the warm brown eyes sparkling with amusement was a sight to file away alongside the cuddling.

Edward yawned and squirmed back down.

"Come on, Mr Wedding Planner, let's get some sleep."

Jamie held his new lover close and then shut his eyes. Sleep pulled him under quickly.

When the dream began it was the usual start. Jamie never understood it fully but he could smell the desert, the sand and the oil from the machinery that supported the Marines, and the dry dusty air. The cursing from other Marines was his soundtrack and he always heard Mikey's distinctive booming laugh. The big guy was his friend, closer than a friend. He was a man who had Jamie's back the same way Jamie had his. This was a patrol of the area the same as any other day. Jamie, Mikey, Rob, Dan, and Oscar were all kitted out and the tastes, scents, and sounds of Afghanistan swirled around them. The early morning air was hot enough to have sweat instant and uncomfortable on the skin, itching and scratching under pale, sand-colored fatigues. This patrol was nothing really. It wasn't the Marines' job to carry out the patrols, but a lost hand of cards and the boredom of waiting for a transport had meant a switch with the soldiers.

It felt good to be walking and focused entirely on the surroundings.

At this point Jamie could usually wake himself up. He didn't want to remember the rest; hell, he wasn't sure his brain had even stored the last twenty seconds of his best friend's life or the death and carnage that he was told had happened. As much as he wanted to wake up there was something in this dream, a steadying hand, a voice telling him to wake up and that it was going to be okay. He felt like he could carry on. The last second, the very moment the air burned around him, played in slow motion. The explosive force of the IED that had been detonated from fuck knows where sent death out in every direction. Jamie remembered the scents had changed to burning and the noises to crying and terror. Mikey was next to him, his face destroyed, the blast catching him first, his body taking some of the destructive power that had been marked for Jamie. All around him his friends were dead, only he lived, only he could carry the memories of his comrades home. For a second or so, he stared up at crystal blue sky and then scarlet red seeped into his eyes, and that was his last memory.

"Jamie…"

Go away. Don't touch me. Just. I don't want to die. Mikey is dead. No, I want to die. I can't breathe. Please just leave me…

"Jamie…"

The panicked, uncertain voice was so different from the medics working on him, the lift as the helicopter took him up and away from the carnage was a discordant noise that cut through the dream, and with a gasp he was awake.

Edward touched him, encouraging him awake with firm words and then reassurances. Sweat coated him and he screwed his eyes tight. What a fucking awesome way to give Edward an insight into Jamie's fucked-up brain.

"That was a bad dream," Edward said gently. He traced the scars on Jamie's chest. "Do you want to talk about it?"

"No," Jamie said immediately. *Hell no.* Talk about the death and destruction and hate and anger thrown at them with the guy who does weddings for a living? How the hell would he understand?

"Try me," Edward said.

"What?" Jamie wasn't following the thread of conversation.

"I may just do weddings for a living but you can use me to get things off your chest."

Jamie groaned. He'd said the wedding thing out loud? Shit. His head hurt and his shoulder ached and his chest felt tight. He fought for a short while over exposing the vulnerability inside him and then common sense kicked in.

"Tylenol," he said.

Edward immediately clambered off the bed and was gone for a short while. Jamie could hear him moving around the room.

"Icy water," Edward finally said. "And two tablets, is that okay?"

Jamie had no choice. He had to sit up and open his eyes. When he did, he got his first glance at take-charge Edward. There was no uncertainty in Edward's face. He looked determined and focused and Jamie took the meds with a swallow of the blessedly cool water. The ice of it chased away the last of the metallic taste in his mouth.

"Does that happen often?"

"Never quite that graphically," Jamie admitted. "I don't think I normally let myself sleep as deeply as that and it chased me down."

"I'm sorry," Edward offered.

"What for? Giving me a chance to sleep? That isn't the issue."

"What is the issue then?" Edward sat down on the end of the bed cross-legged. "Not that you need to tell the Wedding Planner a thing," he added with a smirk.

"Sorry," Jamie said instantly. The heat of embarrassment washed over him.

"Don't be. I'm messing with you. I haven't been where

you've been, or seen the things you've seen, but I've been told I'm a good listener."

"Your voice is gorgeous, you know," Jamie blurted out. "It sounded different in my head when I was in the dream, enough to pull me out." He immediately felt embarrassed again. For a casual hookup, he was handing out an awful lot of his inner self all wrapped up in a bow to Edward.

"Thank you," Edward said cautiously.

"I don't want to talk about what happened," Jamie said firmly. "I've done that over and over and I know the whys and the whens. I lived, others didn't, including my best friend Mikey."

"Oh God, I'm sorry," Edward said instantly. He leaned forward and touched the nearest part of Jamie he could reach, Jamie's arm.

"I have all that shit settled in my head as much as I can. I'm getting stronger every day after they did what they could to keep me alive. I'm back stateside and I have my whole life set out in front of me. Thing is, I have no idea what I want to do with that." He was sitting at an angle so there was no way he could see Edward's face, but suddenly he needed to view the honest reaction he knew he would get from Edward. "I felt like I had no purpose, that I couldn't settle to one thing, and there was absolutely no way I could have a healthy, normal relationship with anyone."

"Why? I mean, hell, not the purpose or anything, but the relationship stuff. You're gorgeous, sexy as hell with a side of rough, and you're exactly right for me at the moment."

The small addition of 'at the moment' made Jamie

suddenly sad, but he ruthlessly pushed it away as a wasted emotion. He wasn't naïve—he knew whatever they had here was defined by the end of Edward's time on the Cay, and anyway, Jamie had a new life to forge.

Self-consciously, he placed a hand flat on his chest and over the scars that would be forever a reminder of that hot dusty day in Afghanistan. The lovers he had before the service were so caught up in the way he looked. They wanted him because he was fit and muscled and strong. Those same men wouldn't want him now.

"I won't be a pity fuck," he said softly. "But—" He stopped and Edward frowned at him. His brown eyes were filled with questions.

"But?" Edward unfolded his legs and shuffled closer. He placed his hand over Jamie's and held it still. "I certainly don't look at you like that."

"I know. That was my *but*. You don't care about these…" He moved Edward's hand to touch the worst of the scarring.

"Nope," Edward said matter-of-factly. "I think they're a sexy badge of honor." He smiled and leaned in for a kiss that Jamie was happy to return. Kissing this prissy, smiling man was getting to be an addiction.

"I'm not a Marine anymore," Jamie said carefully. He tried his hardest to push the uncertainty to one side.

Edward chuckled and gathered Jamie up in a close hug before encouraging Jamie to lie down. "Hell, Jamie, you'll always be a Marine. Thing is, you can be something else as well. An engineer, an architect, a gazebo builder."

"A gazebo builder?" Jamie laughed.

"The world is your oyster."

Jamie shut his eyes tight. He had a smile on his face and he loved that somehow Edward had pulled him out of his nightmare.

"I kind of like the idea of architecture you know," Jamie said softly.

"You could be the first sausage-fingered architect in Miami," Edward said on a yawn. Jamie pulled his new lover close and inhaled the scent of his man.

"You said you liked my fingers." Jamie smiled.

"Love your fingers."

Chapter Eight

EDWARD WOKE UP AND STRETCHED AND THEN RECALLED the reason why he shouldn't be able to stretch fully. Where was Jamie? Probably freaked out over something Edward had said or done. *Great.* Swinging his legs over the side of the bed, he sat up and scrubbed at his eyes. He was disappointed that he had been loved and left. Never mind. Seeing Jamie was going to be awkward from now on but...

Then he saw the note on Jamie's pillow.

"Went for coffee. Meet you in the kitchens."

A goofy smile spread over his face. Coffee with a hot, sexy ex-Marine sounded like his idea of heaven. He grabbed a shower and then stood at his small closet wondering what exactly the well-dressed island man wore to the morning-after-the-night-before meeting with a new lover. Settling on a clean pair of black tailored pants and a fresh white shirt, he dressed quickly. He spent as little time as possible taming his hair and then hurried to the main house and the kitchens. He didn't immediately find Jamie but Dominiq handed him two mugs of heaven in a cup and told him that Jamie was in the walk-in larder area.

Edward went to find him and what he saw had him standing stock still at the door to the large larder room. In the middle of the room sat a rectangular table and all the makings of the cake for the wedding. Jamie was hunched over the small parts that would go to making up the four-tier tower of white that was on the picture to his side. Dominiq had prepared the cakes, iced them in the pure white, and created the strong pillars that would support the layers. The whole thing was to be finished off with flowers, which were currently in the chiller awaiting placement at the last moment.

"Hey," Edward said gently. He didn't want to surprise Jamie if the other man was deep in concentration. Jamie looked up at him and then reached out with a grateful expression on his face for the coffee. Edward handed it to him and was dragged down for a heated kiss.

"Morning," Jamie said. He sounded fresh and not at all sleepy.

"What are you doing?" Edward asked. However much he wanted to be new-not-anal-about-details Edward, he couldn't push away the nerves at seeing Jamie anywhere near his precious cake.

"Building the cake," Jamie said.

"Can you do that?" *Don't let him know you doubt him. Don't go all enraged wedding planner on him.*

"All this is, this cake building, is a form of engineering. No different from building a lookout post in the desert. All this cake will be is an engineering triumph over gravity." Jamie grinned and the smile lit up his face.

Edward couldn't believe he was seeing Jamie in a whole set of interlinked clichés. But time did stop, and he did want to steal every moment of it with Jamie.

"Okay," he finally said.

"Thank you for last night," Jamie said gently. "I don't often get those dreams, but when I do, I sometimes can't get myself out of them." He twisted on the stool, and placing his hands on Edward's thighs, he encouraged him forward until Edward's groin was at eye level, close enough that Jamie had to see how hard he was in his pants. When Jamie nuzzled along the length of his cock with his lips, Edward let out an unmanly sound and then stepped back.

"I can't wait to taste that," Jamie said. There was a question in his eyes. What was he asking for? Reassurance that Edward wanted him? Hope that there would be blowjobs and more in their future? Well, there was no point in wasting time. He'd be gone in three days and Jamie would be off doing architecture or something equally brilliant in whatever job he might choose. May as well fit in as much as he could before then. Quickly, he calculated the time he had at his disposal. He could lose an hour and make it up this evening. He really wanted to feel Jamie's lips on him. *Fuck*. His cock was impossibly hard and he had to focus to actually get words out.

"Build the cake first," Edward said. "Then we need to finish the gazebo, and by my reckoning, give or take a few minutes, we can meet at midday in my room for a siesta."

With a final kiss to Edward's erection through the material of his pants, Jamie turned back to what he was doing. He nodded as he picked up one of the white carved supports.

"Midday. I'm on it."

Edward backed away, lingering in the larder doorway as he watched Jamie return to his careful work. He could happily watch the guy all day. Or he would if he didn't have the exciting little details to tweak in all the guests' bedrooms, the first of whom were due at seven that evening. Smiling, he spun around and held his mug in two hands as he sipped at the hot liquid. These were going to be the longest few hours of his life.

"SO, WHAT DO YOU THINK?" JAMIE FOLDED HIS ARMS across his chest as he nudged Edward's shoulder. The gazebo was finished and if he said so himself, the damn thing looked fucking perfect.

The original roof had survived the rebuild and with a quick lick of white paint, had the whole new-but-old thing going for it. The electricity had passed Scott's scrupulous checks, and the gazebo had passed Edward's.

"Beautiful," Edward said and stepped forward, casting a critical eye over the strings of lights cocooning the gazebo in a romantic glow. "Maybe this one should be a little higher." He adjusted where the lights were hung and then stepped back. "Better. And tomorrow night, with the candles framing the path and steps, it will be perfect."

Jamie looked at the draped lights and tilted his head. It looked exactly the same to him. "Yeah," he lied. "Definitely better."

Proudly, Edward smiled. "I love my job," he said and clutched his oversized diary to his chest.

"What do you keep in that thing?" Jamie asked.

Edward curled his fingers tightly around the bulging spine. "Everything," he stated. "I like to see everything written down. All the details. No surprises."

Nodding, Jamie moved closer. "So, am I in there?" he asked as he rested his hands on Edward's waist and angled him around to face him. "Do you have *this* all mapped out? Day to day?" He smiled and pulled Edward to him. Looking into Edward's eyes, he leaned forward and kissed him. The kiss was slow and sensual, their lips meeting in two gentle pouts as they tasted and teased each other's mouths.

Edward sighed as the kiss ended and then looked up at Jamie with warm brown eyes. "Maybe," he said.

"You don't like surprises?"

He pursed his lips as he seemed to consider Jamie's question. "I don't like the unpredictability of people."

"Unpredictability," Jamie repeated. He smirked as he pushed his groin to Edward's.

Laughing, Edward freed his hand and pressed it to Jamie's chest. "I think this maybe comes under predictable."

"The fact it's quarter past midday and all I want to do is"—he leaned forward to whisper in Edward's ear—"strip you bare, kiss you all over, and have you begging me to stop."

Edward tensed beneath Jamie's touch and looked up through his lashes. "I suppose some surprises are nice." He pushed the nose of his glasses higher as he glanced back at the hotel. There was nobody else around to disturb them. "So, we had midday penciled in." He raised the diary and pressed it to Jamie's chest.

Jamie curled his mouth into a smile. They most certainly did. "Yeah," Jamie said. "We did. But—" He wrapped his hand around Edward's wrist and angled his watch for him to see. "Did I miss my slot?" He wondered how planned to the minute the rest of the day was for Edward.

Grinning, Edward shook his head. "I planned for our time running over."

"Always thinking ahead," Jamie said seductively. "I like that."

"Come on," Edward said and slipped from Jamie's arms. "I have towels to fold into the shape of swans, bubbly to chill, and rose petals to scatter in the guests' bedrooms."

"Sounds exciting," Jamie said and followed Edward as he weaved among the various pots and stones Scott and he had laid out that morning.

Edward shrugged and slowed his pace, waiting for Jamie to fall in beside him. "I like details. I like those little extras that tie a room or a table or whatever together. It may be subtle, it may be crazy extravagant, but people notice. People say everything is perfect and that's because of me."

Jamie wasn't sure he'd seen Edward more passionate about his job than he looked right now. "You're very good at what you do. I mean, everything looks stunning."

Smiling, Edward gave another shrug. "Thanks," he said as they continued to walk. "It took a while to find my feet. Had a few setbacks and had to build my confidence back up, but I like to think I'm good at what I do. I enjoy doing it and love the structure and the organization of the day."

Jamie's gaze drifted downward as Edward spoke, and he drew his lower lip between his teeth as his eyes settled on the curve of Edward's ass. The man wore the skinny, figure-hugging pants Jamie had grown accustomed to seeing him in. Edward was still talking as he opened the door to his room and Jamie dared to reach out and slide his hand into the back pocket of Edward's pants.

Surprised, Edward stopped dead. He raised an eyebrow as he tensed his ass cheek and Jamie squeezed it slightly in return.

"At least you didn't fake a yawn in the back row of the cinema," Edward said sassily. "I mean—"

Jamie pulled Edward close, shutting him up with a kiss as they backed into the room. It didn't take them long to strip away their clothes, undignified and clumsy, between heated kisses.

"Bed," Edward instructed, kicking away his pants and underwear as he pushed at Jamie's chest.

Doing as he was told, Jamie hopped on the bed and pulled Edward with him. They fell together in a tangled mess on top of the bed sheets and Jamie wanted nothing more than to be buried balls deep inside Edward.

Should he be thinking that? Was it too much, too fast?

The space between Edward's legs was warm and inviting, and Jamie nestled between them as he kissed his way across Edward's chest and neck. Edward's skin was sun-kissed and smooth and Jamie just wanted to lick and kiss and mark every inch of the man. Moving higher, Jamie spent some time focusing on Edward's mouth—his full, pink lips and the way they curved as he smiled. Each kiss rushed through him and went straight to the head of his erection. Fuck, he needed to do something, to have Edward fast and dirty and right the fuck now. With only Edward on his mind, he headed south.

"Oh, damn," Edward hissed through clenched teeth as Jamie took him in his mouth. "Sweet Jesus."

Jamie pressed his weight against Edward's thighs as the man arched off the bed. He cupped Edward's balls, pressing delicately against them as he gave them a light squeeze. Hollowing his cheeks, he took the full length of Edward's erection into his mouth, the tip of Edward's dick catching the top of his mouth as he drew him deep inside. He spread his fingers wide across Edward's flat stomach and held him down and then began his determined strokes.

"Mmm," Edward groaned as Jamie quickened his rhythm. Again he tried to raise himself off the bed, to fuck up into Jamie's mouth, but Jamie was the one in control and he wasn't about to relinquish it.

Jamie sucked and licked and teased Edward until his balls were firm in the palm of his hand and his thighs trembled with an excited pleasure. As Edward shifted his weight, parting his legs to maximize his climax, Jamie pulled back, and roughly took Edward's dick in his hand. A few firm strokes and Edward came in heated threads of white across his stomach. Groaning, he tightened his fists in the bed sheets as Jamie continued to tease every last drop of the orgasm until he could take no more.

"Stop," he said and laughed as he pushed Jamie's hand

away from his sensitive length. "Stop." Breathlessly, he dropped to the bed and stared up at the ceiling. "Wow," he managed and danced his fingers through the trail of sticky come across his skin.

Fucking gorgeous. Jamie gazed at the man spread out on the bed beneath him. In the spent, post-sex glow, Edward looked absolutely amazing.

"Shower," Edward said as he held his fingers up toward Jamie. "I need to shower."

Jamie laughed as he sat back on his heels. He had kind of figured it wouldn't take long. "Sure," Jamie said, smacking Edward's ass as he got off the bed.

Edward yelped and grabbed a towel off the dresser. "Back in five," he said and disappeared into the bathroom.

Waiting until the water of the shower started to run, Jamie got off the bed and quickly sought out his jeans. Rifling through the pockets, he found his wallet and looked inside. God love his mother. All through his late teens, she had slipped condoms into his wallet and even now, anytime he left the house, she still did the same damn thing. He had called her on it once, but she simply stated what he knew already, she wanted him to be happy, but she also wanted him to be safe.

He checked the date on the wrapper and then the sachet of lube—silicone based. He grinned. Not so easy to wash away. He turned them over in his hand, and looking to the bathroom door, he listened to the sound of the shower door sliding and the change in the sound of the running water as Edward stepped beneath it.

"What the hell, right?" The worst that could happen

was Edward could tell him to fuck off and stop getting ahead of himself.

Quickly, Jamie got to his feet and made his way to the bathroom. Standing in the doorway, he watched Edward for a moment and gently palmed his dick back to full hardness. The water rolled in enticing streams down Edward's body and tumbled into two routes over the cheeks of his firm, rounded ass. Jamie played with his dick a little more before stepping completely inside and pulling open the shower door.

Edward spun around and wiped the water out of his eyes.

"Thought you might want some company," Jamie said and pulled the door closed behind him. He held up the condom packet and met Edward's eyes. When Edward didn't slap him, he took that as a good sign and moved closer. Soap had left a silky-smooth glaze to Edward's skin and Jamie bit his lip as his dick slid across Edward's thigh and aligned with Edward's.

Edward closed his eyes as Jamie leaned down, kissing a line over his shower-wet skin.

Bending his knees, Jamie traced a line with his tongue down the side of Edward's neck and pressed a kiss below his ear. The man tasted so good and the scent of fresh soap had Jamie's dick twitching at the thought of claiming Edward for his own.

"Okay?" Jamie said and smiled as he held up the condom and lube.

Edward didn't say anything, but took the offered condom. Removing it from the packet, he reached down between them and carefully rolled the sheath down over

Jamie's dick. He met Jamie's eyes as he turned them around, backing himself up against the tiled wall of the shower. Gently, he tugged at Jamie's dick, arching his back off the wall as Jamie slid a hand around behind him and parted his ass cheeks. With a soft grunt, Edward leaned into Jamie, allowing him to tease at his hole with slicked fingers.

Edward raised and lowered his hips, pushing himself back onto Jamie's fingers as he eased them inside. He arched farther back, and Jamie was deeper inside as he stretched and readied him. Jamie wanted to take this slow and concentrate on every inch of Edward. He liked it when lovers took their time with him—focused on the details. He knew how much Edward loved details.

Holding Jamie's face, Edward met him in an openmouthed kiss. Their tongues danced distractingly around each other and Jamie pressed farther and more firmly inside. He smiled into the kiss as Edward made a pleasurable sound and pulled Jamie closer.

Now. It had to be now.

Jamie wrapped his hands around Edward's wrists and pulled them away from his face. Meeting Edward's eyes, he leaned forward for one more kiss before turning Edward around, pressing himself against the man's back, and pinning his wrists to the side of the shower. He gently nuzzled Edward's neck as he rocked his hips, sliding his dick back and forth along the crease of Edward's ass. Edward groaned, his body shivering with what Jamie assumed was anticipation.

"Gonna fuck you. Gonna make you come," he whispered and released one of Edward's wrists as he pushed his dick down and bent his knees, angling himself as he gently eased forward.

Edward spread his legs and shifted his body to allow Jamie better access. Jamie pressed through the ring of muscle into the tight heat that was Edward. A hunger sparked inside Jamie and he reined it in as he allowed Edward time to adjust. Edward was already pushing back, deepening the penetration as their bodies fit together, his ass flush to Jamie's thighs.

Leaning back, Edward rested his head against Jamie's shoulder, and Jamie circled his waist, pulling him back against his solid body as he spread the palm of his hand out over Edward's stomach.

"Okay," Edward groaned and reached up to thread his fingers through the back of Jamie's hair as he turned and tried to capture Jamie's mouth in a kiss. "Okay."

Jamie held Edward tight to him and set a slow pace, gently thrusting forward as the friction slowly lessened and he slid in and out of Edward with more ease. With the acceptance of his intrusion, he quickened his pace, pinning Edward firmly to the wall and trapping his hands. Adjusting his height, he levered himself upward, roughly fucking Edward as his orgasm rose inside him. Not forgetting Edward, he wrapped his hand around Edward's dick, matching his strokes to the rhythm he had set.

Raw sexual sounds rolled from between Edward's parted lips as Jamie pounded into him. Edward was so fucking hot, so astonishingly beautiful, and Jamie was sure he was going to lose it within a minute. He slammed his full weight into the thrust, eliciting more sounds from Edward, who twisted his fingers more tightly in Jamie's hair. The next minute was a haze of thrusts and strokes, and then he came, hot and desperate, as he clung to Edward for all he was worth. Catching his breath, Jamie kissed a line across Edward's water-slick shoulders, roughly bringing him off mere moments later.

Boneless, Edward leaned back against him and Jamie guided him under the spray of the shower, washing away the pattern of sex that had spilled onto both of them.

"That was…" Edward turned around and kissed Jamie, pulling him close as he smiled and then wrapped his arms around Jamie's neck. They stood there for a little while beneath the warm flow of water, simply holding each other. No words, just gentle strokes of their hands over each other's backs.

Jamie held Edward to him and he suddenly found himself not wanting to let go. Closing his eyes, he rested his chin on Edward's shoulder and laid gentle kisses across the man's skin. The Osborne wedding would be over in a few days and then Edward would return to Miami. He ran his lips over Edward's collarbone. A deep sadness filled him as he realized their time together was limited. With Edward, he had been able to push to the back of his mind the reasons he was on the island, the choices he had to make, and the future he had to map out. He clung to Edward like the proverbial life preserver—his life preserver. And letting go was going to hurt a hell of a lot more than he had first thought. He hadn't planned for it, hadn't even seen it coming, but Edward had stolen a place in his heart and he wasn't sure a few days were enough to prepare himself for the space that would be left behind when Edward was gone.

Chapter Nine

JAMIE CROUCHED DOWN NEXT TO DYLAN. "WHAT ARE YOU doing?"

"Checking angles," Dylan said distractedly. He moved to lay flat on his front on the sand and peered through the viewfinder of his camera at something in the distance. He wasn't wearing his usual cutoffs and his hair was tamed with hair gel. Jamie glanced down at his own black pants and tidy white button-down. He wasn't even involved with the wedding but Edward said it was a special day and he wanted to see Jamie all prettied up. His words, not Jamie's. Apparently, looking smart and professional extended even to rough gazebo builders.

He had a message that he needed to give Dylan. "Lucas says there's coffee and a meeting in ten in the kitchen."

Dylan glanced at him. "*Another* Edward meeting?"

"Edward is going through last-minute details."

Scott arrived and crouched down next to Jamie. "What are we all looking at?" he asked curiously.

"Dylan is getting angles," Jamie said helpfully. "I was coming to find you next, we have a meeting in ten."

"You're kidding me. Is this another Edward meeting? That's the fourth one today."

Jamie felt protective of his lover, then flushed when the word lover and Edward in the same thought process had him getting all soft and mushy inside. Everyone assumed the Marine back from Afghanistan would be hard from the outside in, but they couldn't be further from the truth. Somehow Edward was under his skin and Jamie was loving every minute of it.

"He just wants to make sure everything is going to run smoothly," Jamie defended.

"You are so gone on him," Scott said with a laugh.

"Ass," Jamie said with little heat.

"So gone," Dylan added his piece. "I caught you mooning over him. Remember when he was giving us that speech about how the roses needed to be removed from the chill room *exactly* twenty minutes before the ceremony started." Dylan made a kissy face and Jamie thumped him on the arm.

"Says the man who sucks face fifty percent of the day with Lucas. Anyway, I was concentrating because what Edward was saying was important, okay," Jamie said with a nod. "If you get the roses out sooner then they'll wilt in the heat."

"See?" Dylan smiled and clambered to stand. "You were actually listening to one of Edward's talks. Possibly the only one. Everyone knows Edward makes sure he repeats everything again."

Jamie stood and pushed his hands into his pockets. "I

didn't know that. I've only known him four days." And wasn't that the truth. Four days and a couple of hours and he'd fallen into bed with the one guy who had made him feel anything like passion since he was in college. He wasn't sure how he should feel about him and Edward. A casual summer fling was not how he would describe what he had with the Brit. Thing is, this teasing? He'd never been teased about a lover—or whatever Edward was to him—before. Hell, he wasn't used to anyone knowing about him and what he was doing. Feeling like he should leap to Edward's defense was a new one on him.

"We're only messing with you," Dylan said with a grin. "Without Edward we wouldn't have the weddings we have here. He's an expert and I respect that."

"But it's cute the way he can't stop staring at you as well," Scott added.

Jamie looked pointedly at Scott, who backed away laughing.

When the three men arrived at the allotted briefing time Edward was nowhere to be found.

"No Ed?" Dylan asked Lucas. His fiancé shrugged.

"He disappeared, muttering something about napkins. Said he'd be back."

All four of them sat down at the table and one by one the other staff filed in, with Dominiq standing at the back, his arms crossed over his broad chest and his face sweaty with cooking steam. Jamie would hate to be a chef in this island heat. Thank God the wedding itself was taking place at dusk.

"Everyone," Edward announced his arrival with a barked word and all heads turned this way. "T-minus one hour forty. Lucas, front desk, Angie, makeup now, hair is done. Dylan, photos in the bride's room of the preparations." Angie and Dylan disappeared out of the main door, presumably to go find the bride. Lucas followed them. "And, Scott, I need you to get the roses out of the chiller at exactly T-minus twenty."

Scott nodded but he glanced at Jamie with a smirk on his face. Jamie gave him the bird but quickly put his hand down when Edward looked at him over the rims of his glasses. Jamie instantly felt like a kid in a class and pasted an apologetic expression on his face. Then he focused on just how damn hot those glasses looked. At least that meant he wasn't looking at Edward's crotch, which was outlined beautifully in the fitted pants. His shirt today was a dark mustard yellow and his gray tie was perfectly knotted and matched to his gray waistcoat. His hair had that whole volume thing going on which Jamie loved.

Jeez. Stop staring, idiot.

One by one the staff disappeared on various assigned duties until finally it was just Edward and Jamie left in the kitchen.

"What do you need me to do?" Jamie asked. He'd volunteered for anything that put him within touching distance of Edward.

"I need you to kiss me," Edward said quietly. Jamie was suddenly worried. Edward looked pretty calm and unruffled but his words held an edge of desperation. Swiftly, he stood up and pulled Edward into his arms.

"What's wrong?" he asked quickly. In his head he had images of the gazebo in pieces on its side or of candles starting a fire or, hell, a napkin meltdown where they all came unfolded. Then he realized he was belittling what Edward did here and he stopped to think what could really put that odd expression on Edward's face.

Edward sighed noisily. "When I work on a wedding, on the day itself and before, I am one hundred percent focused. But this time... all I can think about since I walked into the kitchen is kissing you. So the way I look at it, I need you to bloody well kiss me until I get it out of my system, and then I can get on with the evening."

"Oh." Jamie managed to get a single word out before Edward placed one hand on his shoulder and leaned in for a kiss. Jamie was happy to get with the plan, and he pulled his lover closer until the diary, Edward's bible, was crushed between them. Jamie tiled his head and deepened the kiss. The taste of his lover was intoxicating, and not for the first time he wondered how he was going to be apart from Edward for any more than a week, let alone staying here when Edward was in Miami.

I want to climb inside this man and stay there for a very long time.

Startled at the stray thought, Jamie released his grip and backed away. Edward still had his eyes closed and his pink lips were shiny from the kiss. He looked peaceful, almost blissed out, and Jamie felt a powerful swell of affection build inside him. Edward was a dangerous temptation all wrapped up in sexy man.

"Better?" Jamie asked. His voice was a little croaky and he realized he was breathing hard. And talking of hard... he reached down and readjusted himself in the slacks then looked down at the slim-fit pants that Edward was wearing.

"Much better," Edward answered.

"You'll need to hide that," Jamie pointed at Edward's groin. Edward grinned and rearranged himself as well.

"I'll just think about the bridegroom's mom." Edward shuddered. "Have you met her?"

"Can't say as I've seen any of the wedding party, actually."

"She pinched my arse," Edward said with a horrified look on his face. He gestured with his arms. "Her ex-husband is standing right next to her, and she pinches me then propositions me." Jamie couldn't help but laugh at the affronted look on Edward's face.

"Just tell her you're gay," Jamie suggested. Edward raised a single eyebrow and then shrugged.

"Like a straight guy could dress as well as me? I thought it was obvious."

With a final kiss on Jamie's forehead he left the kitchen.

"Wait. Edward. What do you want me to do?"

Too late. Edward had gone and Jamie was left in the middle of the large kitchen with no one in sight. He decided he'd go find Scott and see if he could help there. He wanted this to go perfectly for Edward.

Another sign of him completely losing his mind.

———

EDWARD STOOD BACK AND CONSIDERED EVERYTHING ONE last time. There wasn't much he could do now as the service was due to start in T-minus ten. The sun was a scarlet ball of fire low on the horizon and the light had that beautiful eerie quality of dusk. Each candle was lit and the flames steady in the stillness of approaching evening. The gazebo was gorgeous, the metalwork lit by candlelight and the wooden flooring sanded back to expose the grain within. The minister was standing, waiting, and the groom nervously watched the main door where his bride would walk out.

So far Edward had managed to avoid the wandering hands of the mother-in-law-to-be but it had been a near miss when they met on the stairs. Now he just caught glimpses of her staring at him, which unnerved him. The staff were at a discreet distance, and he edged back and away slightly so that one support of the gazebo blocked his line of sight to her. That was probably the right move when he backed into someone who gripped his hips momentarily then released him with a chuckle. Just the touch of Jamie behind him sent the warm and fuzzies flying through his body. He'd never met anyone quite like the Marine with the sadness in his big green eyes.

He didn't regret for one moment taking the step that meant he was in Jamie's bed. Or rather, Jamie was in his bed. Jamie was all take charge one minute then all cuddling and softly spoken words the next. Every touch of Jamie's fingers on his skin was something he prayed for and hoarded for thinking about later. They needed to talk. Was Jamie planning on finding a job on the mainland? Was he planning on staying here on Sapphire Cay? Did he see them maybe meeting up again?

"Okay?" Jamie whispered from behind.

"Bride's ready to go. I have twenty minutes then I move on to reception." Edward leaned back a little until he could feel the body heat from his lover. His presence there calmed him from his usual ceremony nerves. When the bride emerged from the main building and stepped onto the rose-strewn path, Edward knew every single thing he had done to make this day special had been worth it. She was stunning in a lightweight white dress with her ebony hair in curls piled high and speckled with small gems. Her two bridesmaids moved ahead of her then she was there in the gazebo, the candlelight shimmering on her skin and her face wreathed in a smile.

"The best part," Jamie said. He rested a hand on Edward's hip, and Edward had to ruthlessly push down an irrational need to turn and see his lover's face. He had a job to do. He never left anything to chance but he still had to keep his eyes on the ball. He was clearly intoxicated by the beauty and love in his vicinity when all he wanted to do was ask Jamie if he ever wanted forever with another man. He glanced over at Dylan who was taking a respectful few-minute break while vows were spoken, flowery words of love and forever, and Lucas stood with his hand entwined in Dylan's. One day it would be those two having a marriage or a commitment ceremony.

He hoped they exchanged vows here. Envy filtered through him at the thought. Envy followed by irrational hope, which was then chased down by reality. Away from the island he wouldn't be the man Jamie would want to be with. Back in Miami he had a life and he was happy but it was days filled with wedding fairs and suppliers and brides. Not what an ex-Marine would be interested in outside of the romantic Sapphire Cay. On the Cay everything appeared possible.

When the ceremony finished Edward moved inside to orchestrate part two—the wedding meal, speeches, and after.

But when it was all finished, he would spend what was left of his time on the island being with Jamie. He was going to damn well make the most of it.

Chapter Ten

THE DAY HAD BEEN ABSOLUTELY PERFECT AND EDWARD was both emotionally and physically drained. Sitting on a folded blanket, he looked out to the ocean and smiled. Everything he had worked hard for came down to this. This beautiful place and making people's dreams a reality, something they could touch and hold and love.

"Edward," Jamie said from behind him, and Edward looked over his shoulder. "Can I join you?"

Nodding, Edward pulled some of the blanket free from beneath him for Jamie to sit on.

"You okay?" Jamie asked as he crossed his legs and grabbed a handful of dry sand, starting to sift it from one hand to the other.

"Mmm," Edward said and let out a sigh as he closed his eyes and listened. Music echoed down from the hotel, though all he could really make out was the repetitive beat of the current song. He leaned into Jamie and rested his head on his shoulder, reassured as Jamie wrapped his arm around his shoulder and welcomed him into a hug.

They sat for a moment together in silence, just enjoying the closeness as the sounds of the wedding and ocean filled the air.

"You have anything more to do tonight?" Jamie eventually asked.

His work was done and the guests had been left to make their own fun and entertainment for the rest of the evening. "No," Edward said. He'd check on the happy couple tomorrow and make sure everything had been as they'd wanted.

"I was gonna go for a walk. Do you want to join me?"

Edward opened his eyes and looked at the moonlight on the ocean. It was a beautiful night. "You want to go for a moonlit stroll along the beach? How romantic," he teased. "And here I was thinking you were some tough soldier boy."

"Marine," Jamie corrected him and planted a kiss to Edward's forehead. "And it was just an idea. You don't have to make fun of me." His voice sounded serious as he looked away.

Sitting up, Edward shook his head. "I wasn't making fun, or at least I didn't mean to," Edward said as he guided Jamie's face back to his and their eyes met. Edward pouted as he noted the mischievous sparkle in Jamie's eyes. "Now who's taking the piss?"

Jamie laughed and leaned forward, kissing Edward until his pout melted into a smile. "So, walk?" Jamie said. "Maybe find somewhere more private?"

Edward glanced up and down the beach. The guests were all still up at the hotel and there was no one around to disturb them. "We have the whole beach to ourselves," he pointed out.

Jamie nodded and kissed Edward again. "I know, but just think of all that sand and all those places it can crawl up into and—"

"Okay," Edward conceded with a snorted laugh. "Okay." He looked up at Jamie who quickly got to his feet and held out his hand. "Where are we going?" he asked and took Jamie's hand.

Pulling Edward to his feet, Jamie said, "I know somewhere." He grinned and held onto Edward's hand. "Let me show you."

Thoughtfully, Edward looked at Jamie and he couldn't help but think he was getting in far too deep. He shouldn't be wondering what Jamie was thinking, what Jamie wanted, how Jamie felt. Questions like that would have him going insane. No, this needed to stay as a casual thing —lust, not the complications of love.

Shit, no.

He quickly chased the word from his mind. A shag, a fling, a casual thing, he rhymed in his head. *Fuck it*. He was thinking too much—though he kind of liked his little rhyme. "Poet and I didn't know it," he said out loud.

"Edward," Jamie said and pulled on Edward's arm. Puzzled, he looked at Edward. "Poet?"

"Sorry," Edward said and bit his lip. "Been a long day." He squeezed Jamie's hand. "So, what do you want to show me?"

"FOR GOD'S SAKE," EDWARD SNAPPED AS HE STUMBLED forward through the overgrown greenery.

Jamie chose to ignore Edward, just like he had the last fifteen times. He totally wasn't keeping count.

"When you start engineering, I think your first job should be to have at that tree."

Jamie stopped and raised an eyebrow, looking up at the tree Edward had threatened. "What have trees got to do with engineering? Anyway, it's a kapok tree and it's very old." Smirking, he reached out and took some fallen debris from Edward's hair. "I think it likes you." He held out the feathery fiber to Edward.

Sighing, Edward pushed away Jamie's hand and walked past him. "Is it much farther?"

"No," Jamie said and jogged a few steps to catch up with Edward. "This way." He took Edward by the hand again and swerved off to the left. The trees thinned out and eventually the two of them stepped out into a clearing.

"Where are we—" Jamie pressed his finger to Edward's mouth, shutting him up. "What?" Edward whispered.

"Listen," Jamie simply said.

He kept his eyes on Edward, watching as the man narrowed his eyes as he listened. "I don't hear anything," Edward said.

"Just shut up and listen," he instructed, trying hard not to laugh as Edward scowled at him like a reprimanded teenager. "Do you hear it?"

Edward tilted his head and shrugged. "Water?" he said.

Jamie nodded. "There's a spring that fills this pool back there and it's set against the rocks."

"Really?" Edward said. "No one's ever said."

"That's because it's a secret. My mom and dad came here a lot when they were younger. The rocks can be slippery and it's a bit of a trek."

Edward looked back over his shoulder and smoothed a hand over his hair. "You can say that again."

"Come on," Jamie said and crossed the clearing, making his way through the line of trees.

Abruptly, he stopped and caught Edward, steadying him after he bumped into him. They both stared at the illuminated pool.

"It's like walking in on your parents," Edward said loudly.

"Edward," Lucas said as he pushed Dylan's arms from around him and jumped sideways through the water with a splash. "Jamie." His hands disappeared beneath the surface of the water and Jamie knew exactly what he was covering.

"Guys," Dylan said and waded through the water toward his trunks, which were spread out on one of the rocks.

Jamie turned his back and nudged Edward to do the same.

Edward put his hand on his hip and rolled his eyes. "Okay," he whined, glancing at the two men in the pool before joining Jamie in looking away.

They waited as Lucas and Dylan splashed in the water, getting their trunks on and talking between themselves in low voices.

"You can turn around now," Dylan said.

"Hey," Lucas said and Edward and Jamie turned

around. "Didn't expect to see you two tonight." The man looked so embarrassed and color heated his face. Dylan on the other hand, looked at ease as he leaned back in the water and let himself float on the surface.

Though he tried not to, Jamie couldn't help but notice the outline of Dylan's erection beneath the clinging, wet material of his trunks. "Sorry," he said and did his best to focus on Lucas. "I didn't think we'd see anyone out here." He looked at the lanterns surrounding the pool. "Sorry," he apologized again.

"No worries," Dylan said, moving his hands in circles as he kept himself afloat in the water.

"Sure." *Well this isn't awkward at all.*

Lucas simply smiled up at them as he gravitated toward Dylan's side.

"Anyway, we should probably head back," Jamie managed and looked at Edward. "It's been a long day, and gee, I'm beat." A comical expression passed over Edward's face as he shook his head. "What?"

"Nothing." Edward raised his hand. "Have a great evening," he said to Lucas and Dylan and wrapped his hand around Jamie's wrist, pulling him back toward the trees.

"See you at breakfast," Dylan called after them, and laughter and splashing could be heard as they walked away.

"Gee, I'm beat?" Edward said and laughed. "You are so adorable."

Jamie let Edward guide him back toward the clearing and then pulled him close into a hug. "And you are amazing," he said and kissed him.

Gently, he squeezed his arms around Edward's waist and held him in a warm embrace, lifting him slightly from the ground as he leaned back and teased Edward's mouth with his tongue. "So, what now?" he whispered between kisses.

Edward smiled as he was lowered back to the floor and circled his arms around Jamie's neck. "Now we have to decide."

"Decide what?"

With a grin, Edward teased Jamie's earlobe before saying, "Your place or mine?"

THE MORNING AFTER THE NIGHT BEFORE AND EDWARD JUST wanted to crawl under a quilt and sit in the dark for a little while. After all the stress and all the preparation of the wedding day, the day after was like some huge downer. Sitting on the edge of the bed, he stared at his phone. Marylou-Beth had been in touch to confirm his flight for tomorrow and he felt conflicted. He hadn't had a chance to really talk to Jamie about whether this thing of sex and cuddles and easy conversation was heading anywhere. Would Jamie want to hook up again here or maybe in Miami? Was it just about the sex and snuggling? Or could there be a future for them?

His cell ringing dragged him from his thoughts. "Lucas," he said as he answered the call. "Everything okay?"

"Where are you?"

"My room. Why?"

"Erm, no, you're not," Lucas said with a laugh.

Edward looked around, blinking as the room came into focus. He had gone back to Jamie's for the first time last night. Jamie had headed out early with Scott to Marsh Harbor and he had been on the phone to Marylou-Beth since then. "Yeah, sorry. I'm not awake. What did you need?"

"Just had some paperwork that needed signing before you leave. Are you going later today?"

"Tomorrow," he confirmed. *Shit.* He really needed to pin Jamie down and have a conversation.

Lucas said, "Well, stop by the office later, yeah? You can check the details for the end of November and the Greenway wedding."

"Sure," Edward said.

There was a pause before Lucas asked, "Everything okay?"

"Yeah, of course. Why wouldn't it be?" Edward said. He knew he sounded snappy.

"I'll see you later," Lucas said and hung up.

Crap. He must have sounded like some pissy, whiny bitch —a bigger one than usual. He needed to get up, get dressed, and bury himself in trivial things like color swatches for seat covers. He couldn't sit around forever waiting for Jamie to get back. Getting to his feet, he picked up his pants from last night. A shower, a change of clothes, fix his hair, and grab something to eat, and Edward would feel a hell of a lot better. With that positive thought taking over, he got dressed and headed back to his room. He was going to push thoughts of Jamie from his mind and make the most of his day.

· · ·

A COUPLE OF HOURS PASSED AND HAVING CHECKED THAT everything was okay with the wedding party, Edward headed to find Lucas.

Knocking, Edward stuck his head around the door and looked into the office. Lucas was sitting at his desk, his feet resting on a second chair as he leaned back and stretched his arms above his head.

"Working hard?" Edward said as he stepped into the room and looked around. He had never grasped how Dylan or Lucas could work in the small office. It was a mess, organized chaos Dylan claimed. Paper bulged out of open drawers, a mug had left a circular stain on the wooden desk, the windows didn't look like they had been cleaned in a few years, and the ceiling fan made a strange rattle as it spun above them.

"Always," Lucas said and sat up, lowering his feet as he dragged his chair closer to the desk. He smiled as he sorted the papers on his desk into a single pile and then indicated the seat opposite him. "Everything went okay yesterday?"

Edward nodded as he perched on the edge of the seat and folded his arms across his diary. "Yes. They're here for two weeks, so that's over to you to look after. Oh and Dylan will need to set up a session to talk photographs and albums with them."

"I'll make sure he remembers," Lucas said and picked up the top paper, holding it out to Edward. "These are the last details we had for the Greenways. Just wanted to confirm everything was up to date and also hoped you'd sign this." He picked up a second page.

"What's this?" Edward looked at the sheet of paper and

a smile spread across his face. "When?"

Lucas smiled. "Not for a couple of years, but I know you get busy and well, we want the best."

Edward's heart swelled with pride. "Will it be here on the island?" From the moment he had heard about Dylan's proposal, he'd always had a tinge of jealousy. Even with the number of weddings he had organized in his few years in the business, he had never really thought about getting married himself one day. He was always so focused on making everyone else's dreams come true.

Shrugging, Lucas sat back. "I don't know," he said honestly.

Edward pursed his lips thoughtfully. Though the island was a special paradise for all his brides and grooms, Lucas and Dylan lived here together most of the year. It maybe didn't hold that same enchantment it used to.

Excitedly, he opened his diary to the notes page. "When were you thinking?"

Lucas laughed. "We really didn't get beyond agreeing we wanted you to do it."

"Oh," Edward said, a little disappointed. "Okay." He closed his diary. "We can sort out the deposit when you're sure if you'd prefer?"

Lucas shook his head. "No, we're sure we want to get married."

Edward smiled. "No, I meant sure of a date."

"Ah," Lucas said and blushed. Edward loved the innocent charm Lucas always seemed to have.

"I'll tell you what," Edward said and picked up a pen off Lucas's desk. He signed his name at the bottom of the contract and then pressed the pen nib against the blank space for the date. "Once you decide, get in touch. We'll fill this in and I'll put you in my book." Lucas smiled knowingly. Edward's diary was his life and Lucas had had to comfort Edward through the last meltdown when the diary had been misplaced. They never had figured out how it had ended up in the ladies' bathroom down in reception.

"Thank you."

Edward gave an easy shrug. As if he'd have said no. He loved Dylan like some strange twice-removed cousin whom he saw on birthdays and during the holidays. And Lucas, he was so sweet, it was enough to make his teeth ache.

"So, what's going on with you?" Lucas moved the conversation on.

"Me? I have just taken on an Indian extravaganza to plan for May. I need to start chasing up the Greenways for next month and to talk favors with two lovely ladies who marry in three weeks—each other, that is." He took off his glasses and cleaned the lenses. Putting them back on, he was met with an amused expression from Lucas. "What?"

"I meant…" Lucas scratched the back of his neck. "I meant, with you and Jamie."

Him and Jamie? Was that how everybody saw them? Edward-and-Jamie. Jamie-and-Edward.

"We're…" What the hell were they? Lucas looked at him expectantly. "We're just friends. Throw in the benefits bit and that's us."

"So, it's not serious?"

Edward shrugged. "I wouldn't go telling my mother to buy herself a new hat or anything. It's just a bit of fun. Killing time."

The look on Lucas's face quickly made Edward doubt what he was saying. "He seems like a nice guy," Lucas said. "I'm sure he appreciates your *friendship*."

Please don't get me thinking on Jamie again. He'd had a great morning not thinking about the tall, tanned, handsome, muscular, gazebo-building hunk of a man. Edward groaned inwardly. *Fuck it.* Yes, Jamie was all kinds of hot but he was also sensitive, loving, and Edward had this thing about hurt puppies and wanting to smother them in cuddles and keep them safe.

He needed to call Marylou-Beth again and have her talk him down. If anyone could put him off men and this man in particular, it would be her. She had more failed romances than any girl should have had in her thirty-one years, and if anyone could steer him in the right direction and away from the stoic muscle man it would be her.

"I have to go and do stuff," Edward said and knew he sounded ridiculously pathetic.

Lucas met his eyes and nodded. "Okay. What time is your flight tomorrow? I'll arrange with Scott to take you over."

"The flight's at one twenty." Edward got to his feet.

"Okay. We'll get you there in good time."

Edward held his diary to his chest. "Thanks," he said. He guessed the countdown had begun. T-minus twenty-four hours.

Chapter Eleven

JAMIE JUMPED DOWN OFF THE SMALL BOAT AND TIED THE
rope, then turned back to assist Scott with unloading the
boxes of supplies. With the two of them working on it the
job didn't take long, and between them they transported
everything up to the main house.

"Did you get my tomatoes?" Dominiq said quickly.
Jamie thought the chef had been standing in reception
waiting for them and he immediately reassured the big
man. Clearly, tomatoes were an item that was important
to him.

"Everything you asked for," he said.

"You're an angel," he said dramatically. Then he pulled
Jamie into a bear-crushing hug and Jamie immediately
hurt. He didn't say anything. Just went with the hug and
waited for Dominiq to pull back. He moved away and
grabbed up the two bags of fresh produce, muttering
something about chillers and soup.

"You okay?" Scott asked. He stood directly in front of
Jamie and stared at him, concerned.

"Yes," Jamie said quickly. His instant reflex was to always reassure people that yes, he was fine. He was lying. His chest scars had protested at the tight hold and suddenly he felt pathetically not-okay at all. It felt like the muscle was in spasm.

"Your hand is on your chest," Scott observed. "You're not going to have a heart attack on me, are you?"

Jamie thought on his feet. "Wasn't me who ate three burgers and two fudge sundaes at the harbor." He smirked.

Scott looked around worriedly. "Shh, if Dominiq hears…"

The two men laughed and Jamie made a conscious effort to compartmentalize the pain that radiated from his scar and out to his side. Just until he got back to his room and got some muscle relaxants. This didn't happen often but when it did, he told anyone curious that he had a migraine.

People understood migraines.

Jamie pushed through the chores he needed to complete, only stopping when the pain radiated into his shoulder and left his right arm numb and tingling. He stopped in at Lucas and Dylan's office. The room was in its usual chaos and he wondered if Edward had ever been inside it. His OCD probably hated that nothing appeared to have order. The guys could do with more shelves and maybe a couple of custom-built storage units. He could do that before he left. He had a few weeks to kill. Lucas sat in the middle of it all with what looked like accounts sheets spread around him.

"Taking the rest of the afternoon off, if that's okay."

Lucas looked up and blinked owlishly. "You don't

work here, Jamie," he smiled. Then he frowned. "You look like shit."

"Starting a migraine," Jamie lied.

"Do you need anything? I used to have migraines. Do you have any Excedrin?"

"Yes." Jamie wasn't sure what that was but assumed it alleviated migraines. "I just need sleep."

"Of course. Go. Go lie down."

Jamie left and made his way down the path to his place and hoped to hell he didn't meet anyone else. He needed his muscle relaxants and his bed and by tomorrow he'd be fine. Thereafter he would attempt to avoid bear hugs from Dominiq. He didn't even want to begin to think how easy it had been to disrupt the fragile strength in his chest. Icy cold water smoothed the way for the medication, and after pushing just his jeans off, he crawled into bed. Finding a comfortable position would be hard. The numbness in his arm was now a throbbing ache and the pain in his chest was making it hard to breathe. That was the kicker. If his breathing became too shallow then he wouldn't be able to relax because he'd be concentrating so damn hard on the inhalation and exhalation that he needed to calm. He hoped he'd taken the meds in time.

It took a while but the moment the Baclofen kicked in he could feel his muscles relaxing. He placed a hand over the worst of the scar tissue. His dog tags lay there and he grasped them and held tight. He'd come home alive. He was good. He worked most days and he didn't have the PTSD that other survivors had. *I'm strong and most of all, lucky.*

Wriggling, he found a more comfortable position then

he began to count back from a hundred until sleep took him.

WHEN HE WOKE THE FIRST THING HE REALIZED WAS THAT IT was dark. The second was he wasn't alone.

"Hey, sleepyhead," Edward said softly.

"Whattimeissit?" he hissed. His mouth was dry and nausea washed over him.

"Just after eleven. I've been watching you sleep."

"Creepy," Jamie attempted to joke.

"I was worried," Edward informed him. He was lying on the bed next to Jamie and he passed a glass of water over from the cabinet. "Lucas said you had a migraine."

At this point here Jamie could just say yes. He was tempted to. He wasn't likely to see Edward for a while and by the time they saw each other again—if they did— Jamie's chest would be even stronger than it was now. He'd not need to see any frailty or a chink in Jamie's armor. All Jamie had to do was say yes. Telling Edward the truth meant placing one hell of a lot of trust in the other man. He didn't think Edward was with him just because he was an ex-Marine. He'd evidently seen something hot and interesting under the scars.

"It wasn't a migraine," he said finally. Edward shifted in the bed and turned on his side to face Jamie.

"What was it?" he asked quietly.

Jamie took his hand and entwined their fingers. He then placed them over his heart. "Dominiq hugged me. The guy doesn't know his own strength and he took me by surprise."

"Did Dominiq make a pass?" Edward said. He sounded confused but the thought of the big married chef making a pass at him was pretty funny and Jamie couldn't help but release the small huff of a laugh.

"No," Jamie protested. "He hugged me because of the tomatoes."

"That makes perfect sense," Edward said dryly.

"I was standing awkwardly, probably breathing in, and he hugged me tightly. The muscle weakness I have started up with all its usual shit."

"Like?"

"Spasm, which is painful, and it goes out to my arm."

"But you did the gazebo, and I made you stretch and hang all those lights—"

"Don't," Jamie said firmly. "Ninety-nine percent of the time I'm fine. Just, I didn't walk away with a bandage on a small cut. My right lung was wrecked, but they saved what they could and every day it gets better. But I may have this issue for the rest of my life." With his free hand he reached to the cabinet next to the bed and located his Baclofen. "These would knock out a horse," he said. He dropped them on his chest and looked down at their joined hands over his scars and the medication sitting there.

"Okay," Edward offered. Jamie couldn't bring himself to turn his head to look into Edward's eyes. He wondered what he would see in their brown depths. Edward was a good guy but Jamie didn't want pity or crap like that.

"Yeah," Jamie said, just to fill the silence.

"Well that's fucked up," Edward said gently. "Do you have physio? Exercises to do?"

"Yeah. A whole load of them."

"Good. Is it getting any better at all?" Edward squeezed Jamie's fingers.

"What is this?" Jamie asked crossly. "Twenty questions?"

"I just want to know so I don't hurt you when we're in the middle of the hot-heavy-sweaty-sex part of this relationship," Edward countered.

Jamie turned his head immediately to face Edward. There was still not one ounce of pity in his lover's eyes. Just interest. "Really? You're going with the sex angle?" Jamie was a little surprised but relieved as the weight lifted from him.

"We have good sex," Edward murmured. He pressed a kiss to Jamie's covered chest then another.

"Not tonight we don't," Jamie said seriously.

Edward looked up at him through long, dark lashes and pretend pouted. Then he smiled. "You ready for more sleep?"

Jamie yawned as if by command then nodded. The meds lingered and hell, he was tired. Edward untangled his fingers from Jamie's and leaned over to switch off the small lamp. Then he snuggled as close as he could without actually touching Jamie and yawned himself.

"I am more than happy to sleep if I get to do it next to you," he said softly.

"You can get closer," Jamie replied.

Edward moved a little closer, his body warm and his scent so familiar. Jamie could lay here forever with Edward's breathing evening out and the darkness hiding everything until morning.

God, he was going to miss Edward when he went.

. . .

Jamie passed the final box to Scott.

"How many bags does one wedding planner have?" Scott teased. Edward glared and continued with his listing off of everything he needed to get back to the office.

Files, supplies, chair covers—in fact three boxes of stuff that had Scott huffing and puffing in the midday heat.

"One can't bring off simply wonderful weddings without one's boxes," Lucas deadpanned in an awful fake British accent.

"Ha bloody ha," Edward said. His lips twitched with holding back a laugh and Jamie fell a little bit more for the intriguing man who had been sharing his bed and his dreams for six days.

"Aww, leave him alone," Dylan interrupted. "He can't help his accent."

"I think it's cute," Jamie interrupted, then wished he hadn't. Scott stared at him with a smirk. Dylan and Lucas exchanged glances and were clearly trying not to laugh or say something or whatever. Edward smiled at him and took the two steps to get closer. He placed his hands on Jamie's shoulders and squeezed gently.

"Well, that is all that matters."

Scott made kissy noises and Edward released his hold to flash Scott the finger. Then he placed a very gentle kiss to Jamie's lips. They had said their goodbyes this morning. Jamie felt better, although still sore, and they had kissed and hugged. Their final hour together had been more peaceful and quiet than the monkey sex Edward had suggested before. Jamie wasn't going to

Marsh Harbor; they'd decided that just a few minutes before.

"Can we get some privacy?" Edward asked on a sigh. Lucas and Dylan both hugged him then walked away back to the house. Scott sat cross-legged in the boat and focused on the far horizon.

"I'll see you when I get back for the next wedding," Edward whispered.

"A month and two days," Jamie confirmed.

"Come with me today. Stay with me," Edward suddenly said.

Jamie wasn't ready for the city yet. He wanted more healing. He wanted the time between meds to lessen—hell, he wanted to be normal. While he would never be entirely healed, he wanted the space to think about what he wanted to do.

"I'm staying here for a while longer."

Edward nodded then rested his forehead against Jamie's. "I know. I'm going to miss your sausage fingers."

This made Jamie laugh, and at least when Edward climbed aboard the boat Jamie didn't feel like this was an end. Edward said he wanted more, and Jamie was definitely interested.

Just not right now.

He stood in the same position until the boat was long gone. At some point Lucas reappeared at his side.

"You're going to miss him," he said.

"Yeah. I'd kind of gotten used to him."

"Seems to me it was quite a bit more."

"He's back in a little over a month."

"Yeah, the Greenway wedding," Lucas confirmed.

"Big themes and a lot of work. Will you still be with us then?"

Jamie remembered he had never actually said how long he would stay. When he'd arrived it had only been to visit for a while, but he hadn't realized how much he needed this island.

"If that's okay," he said.

Lucas nodded. "More than okay. Want a beer?"

That sounded like a great idea. Together they walked to the house. Jamie was lost in thought. A month was a long time for Edward to come to his senses and realize Jamie wasn't a good bet as a lover.

Still, he'd have to take that chance. A month was also a nice long time for Jamie to get his head straight about what he wanted to do next.

The beer was cold, the air was warm, and Lucas and Dylan pulled him out of his melancholy thoughts with stories and jokes and everything he needed at that moment.

God, he missed Edward.

Chapter Twelve

"YOU GOT A MINUTE?" JAMIE ASKED AND STEPPED INSIDE the hotel office.

Dylan scratched a hand through his shaggy hair as he stretched in the battered leather seat. "Sure," he said with a smile.

Jamie had been thinking on this for eight days—eight very long and strange days. He couldn't remember the last time anyone had gotten in his head and under his skin as much as Edward had managed to.

"What's up?" Dylan leaned forward and eyed Jamie with interest.

How could he say this? "I'm heading back to the mainland." Okay, that came out easier than he had thought it would.

"Okay," Dylan said. "We can arrange that."

Really? It was as simple as that?

Dylan must have noticed how unsure Jamie looked. "There's no contract. It's not a problem."

"I just didn't want you to think I didn't appreciate everything you've done this last month. For letting me come back here."

It was clear from the expression on Dylan's face that this was a non-issue. "I just hope it's helped." He pursed his mouth thoughtfully. "Has it?"

"You have no idea," Jamie said and looked at his feet. Yes, he still hurt and his road to recovery still had a way to go, but inside, in his head, things were clearer, calmer.

Dylan got out of his chair and walked around his desk. "So, what are you going to do?"

Now there was a question. He had a plan. A slightly open-ended plan, but a plan nonetheless. "Head back to Miami, stay at my parents' place for a while, find some work." He'd found a couple of relevant courses to his interests in architecture engineering and even landscaping. Perhaps he could even go to night classes to help him decide what he really wanted to do.

Nodding, Dylan leaned back against the edge of the desk and folded his arms across his chest. "Well, I won't say we won't miss you, because we will. You've been a great help."

Jamie gave a breathy laugh. "Thanks," he said. Compliments had never been an easy thing for him to accept.

They stood together, an awkward silence hanging between them until Dylan finally broke it. "Right, I've got to ask, because Lucas will kill me if you leave and he doesn't find out."

"Ask?" Jamie wondered. "About?"

"Edward."

Edward. Jamie worried his lip and pushed his hands in the pockets of his oversized hoodie. He had thought about it and wondered how the wedding planner would receive him. "He's in Miami," Jamie stated the obvious.

Dylan nodded. "Yes, he is. And?"

Jamie simply shrugged. Feelings and all that shit, Jamie hated talking about himself. Besides, why did Dylan and Lucas even care what happened once he left the island?

Smiling, Dylan rocked back against the edge of his desk. "Okay." He wasn't going to press, and for that Jamie was thankful. "Do you have a flight booked?"

"Yeah," Jamie said. "This evening."

"Okay," Dylan said again and stepped forward, surprising Jamie and pulling him into a brief hug. Patting Jamie's back, Dylan then released him. "Just promise me one thing." He looked at Jamie and pointed toward his chest. "Trust this, yeah? And follow your heart." His eyes brightened. "Lucas taught me that."

Follow his heart. Jamie nodded. He could do that.

"Come here," Lucas said and dragged Jamie into a warm hug as they stood on the small pier beside the boat. "You got everything?"

Jamie relaxed into the hug and tried to ignore the pressure against his chest. Seriously, the two men weren't much older than him and yet the goodbye felt like two dads waving their son off to college.

"I think so." Jamie stepped back as Lucas released him. Though he had arrived with one bag, he had somehow managed to gain two more. One was filled with various personal items he had collected during trips to the mainland and the other was crammed with treats Dominiq had cooked up for him.

"Well, if we find anything we'll mail it on. Though, you're always welcome to come back anytime." Lucas grinned. "Dylan needs all the help he can get," he added.

Dylan playfully swatted Lucas's arm and then looked at Jamie. "You ready?" he asked.

Jamie looked back up at the hotel in the low light and took a deep breath. This had been his home, his haven for the last month. This place was his past, though, and it was time to make himself a future.

"Yeah," Jamie finally said. He picked up one of his bags as Dylan collected the other two and headed onto the boat.

"Oh," Lucas said suddenly and stepped forward. "This is for you." He held out a folded envelope. "Just in case."

Taking the envelope, Jamie pushed it in his jeans pocket. He'd look at it on the ride to Marsh Harbor. "Thanks," he said, giving a shy nod as he turned and boarded the boat. He took his seat and waited as Dylan started the engine. He was going to miss the island and the people. Lucas and Dylan had made the island their own, but all the familiar memories of his childhood were still there for him to find—beauty, warmth, peace, and most importantly, the sense of home and family.

The boat lurched forward and Jamie looked over his

shoulder one more time. He was going to miss Sapphire Cay, but he needed to move on. He needed get his life back on track. Turning around, he focused on the dark ocean in front of them and the landmass on the horizon. *Time to look forward*, he told himself and reached into his pocket for the envelope Lucas had handed him. Opening it, he looked inside and narrowed his eyes. All that was inside was a small card. He took the card and snorted a laugh as he found it was a business card. Blush Pink. He ran his thumb over the interlinked hearts in the top corner of the card and then downward over Edward's name and the Miami address for his office.

Jamie looked up as Dylan glanced over his shoulder. Tapping the card thoughtfully against his chin, Jamie considered the British wedding planner—*his* British wedding planner. He smiled as he wrapped his hand around the card. They had left it as a see-you-at-the-next-wedding kind of thing. Had Edward meant it when he had asked Jamie to go back to Miami with him?

Returning the card to the envelope, he pushed it back into his pocket. Edward wasn't the only thing on his mind at the moment—first were a job and his own place. He needed to step back and deal with one at a time. Either that or he was pretty sure he was going to drive himself insane thinking about it all at once. First thing, get settled at his folks, then see about the jobs on offer in Miami and then, then he'd get to Edward.

Resting his chin on his hand, he watched the ripple of the ocean's surface and smiled. The future suddenly seemed a hell of a lot better and bigger than he could ever have hoped for. He was going to be okay. He really was.

"PEACH," EDWARD SAID AND RAN THE RIBBON THROUGH his hand. "I hate peach."

"Sweetie, the bride, or brides in this case, are always right. You give them what *they* want." Marylou-Beth took the ribbon from his hand and flattened it out across the desk between them. "It's not so bad."

"It's old-fashioned."

"It's traditional," Marylou-Beth quickly retorted.

Sighing, Edward conceded. Dealing with two brides had been a bigger nightmare than he had thought possible. The women were headstrong and knew exactly what they wanted, which wouldn't usually be a problem except for the fact they had shockingly bad taste in apparently everything.

"Okay," he said and opened his diary. His to-do list for this wedding was getting out of hand. He really needed to let go and let Marylou-Beth take on a little more before he had a full-blown meltdown. "I need you—" Marylou-Beth gave him a startled look. "Yes, *you,* to meet with Veronica and Jo and handle all the final payments on the room, the DJ, and the photographer." She looked a little pale. "Okay?"

"Uh-huh," she said, nodding.

"Good." Edward took a deep breath. He felt strangely better. Marylou-Beth wore a different expression as he looked at her. She stared over his shoulder and the look in her eyes changed from suspicion to interest to *hottie in the room.* Narrowing his eyes, Edward twisted in his seat and looked over his shoulder. To say his jaw almost hit the floor was an understatement.

"Holy hell," he said and quickly got out of his chair. Taking the few short steps, he bounded across the room and into Jamie's hold. He wrapped his arms around Jamie's neck and pulled him close. God, he had missed the feel of holding the muscular Marine tight. *Shit. Too tight.*

Edward jumped back as if Jamie was on fire. "Are you okay? Did I hurt you?" He scanned Jamie's face looking for any indication that he had hurt the man.

Jamie shook his head. "I'm fine." He smiled warmly and clearly appreciated Edward's unnecessary concern. He rested a hand on the back of Edward's neck and pulled him toward him. "I'm fine," he said again and kissed Edward on the mouth. The kiss was gentle and Jamie's mouth was soft and warm. "I missed you."

Leaning back, Edward smiled. "I missed you too." He ran his hands up Jamie's biceps and over his strong shoulders.

Jamie tilted his head and looked at him curiously.

"Just checking," Edward said. "You're really here." The feel of Jamie beneath his hands was incredible. He had missed Jamie more than he had dared to admit, even to himself. He met Jamie's eyes and asked, "Why are you here?"

He didn't mean to sound rude or anything, but he had never expected Jamie to just show up at the office.

Jamie kissed him again and grinned. "Don't ever change," he said.

With a sigh, Edward took Jamie by the hand and turned

around. Marylou-Beth had a ridiculous grin slapped on her face. "Marylou-Beth, this is Jamie."

"Hi," she said as she got to her feet and held out her hand. "I've heard a lot about you."

Jamie shook her hand and then looked suspiciously at Edward.

"All good," Marylou-Beth chirped in. "I promise. Though," she said and took her seat, "he's been a little distracted this last week. Seems he's had other *things* on his mind."

Oh, you do not want to try and out-sass me. Edward shot her a look and Jamie laughed. "Oh look, it's lunchtime. See you in an hour." He guided Jamie by the shoulder through to the back office and shut the door on his openmouthed assistant.

Jamie laughed. "I guess that answered my next question."

"What?" Edward asked as he sat on the edge of his pristine and tidy desk.

"If you were free for lunch." He stepped forward and rested his hands on Edward's waist, gently easing him backward to sit more fully on the desk.

What Jamie's touch did to him... Edward opened his legs as Jamie slid into the space between them. "What are you doing here?" he asked. His voice was softer this time as he draped his arms over Jamie's shoulders.

"I came to see you."

Edward rolled his eyes and sighed. "I meant, why are you in Miami? I thought you were staying on the island. I thought you needed more time—" Jamie shut him up with a kiss and Edward closed his eyes as Jamie pulled him forward, pressing their groins together, hot and hard. So damn hard. They stayed like that for a few minutes, kissing and holding each other until finally the need for air overcame them.

Opening his eyes, Edward looked up at Jamie. The man certainly looked more peaceful and rested than when they first met. He held Jamie's face and looked deep into the green depths of his eyes. Yes, he looked better.

"I got back a few days ago," Jamie confessed. "I would have come sooner but I had so much to do. I didn't want to see you until I was settled. Sorry."

Edward shook his head. "You don't need to apologize."

With a shrug, Jamie pressed his crotch more firmly to Edward's. "You mean a lot to me. More than I realized."

Gently, Edward soothed lines over Jamie's cheeks and jaw. "Glad to hear it," he said and leaned forward to kiss Jamie. Slowly at first, he kissed and teased and tasted the man's mouth, until desire took over and the kiss became hungry and heated. Their hands wandered, sensual touches turning to desperate pulls at clothing until both men had lost their shirts and Edward's pants were hanging loosely off his hips.

Muscles rippled in Jamie's arms and shoulders as he lifted Edward off the table and struggled to pull his underwear lower. Freeing the material, Jamie lowered Edward onto the desk, nudging him back and leaning over him as he kissed lines across his chest and stomach.

The feel of Jamie's mouth across his body was dizzying and Edward desperately wanted more. It had barely been two weeks, but Edward had missed feeling this, having someone, so damn much. Edward groaned, his thoughts focusing solely on Jamie as the man slipped his hand into his clothes and between his legs, taking his erection in his hand and applying pressure in steady strokes.

"I fucking love you," Jamie growled against Edward's chest.

Edward opened his eyes and looked up at his office ceiling. *Well, shit.* He needed to answer that. Was Jamie looking for the words? Was he even sure about what he felt? They'd only had a few days on the island really, but hell, he'd missed him. Jamie didn't seem to be waiting for a response—he was kissing and tasting. Edward pushed aside the need to think. He couldn't stop now. Pulling himself up, he reached between them, fighting to free space so he could get inside Jamie's clothes. He held onto Jamie with one hand and distracted the man with kisses. Finally, with Jamie's dick in his hand, hot, hard, and thick, Edward struggled to stave off his rising orgasm.

Not yet.

The next few minutes were a rush of touches and kisses and rough fucking into each other's hands. Edward came first with a muted cry and clung to Jamie for dear life. Moments after, he brought Jamie crashing over the edge into his own orgasm and the two rested boneless and uncomfortable against each other.

"I hope Marylou-Beth went to lunch," Edward said and laughed as he leaned back and lay across his desk. He turned his head and looked at the slightly disheveled pile of paper. He really should fix that. His lover running his hands over his chest regained Edward's attention. He looked up at Jamie and smiled. "Did you mean it?"

Jamie continued to rub his warm hands across Edward's chest. "Mean what?" Jamie asked and leaned forward to kiss Edward's right nipple.

Don't come off as needy. "You said you loved me."

Leaning back, Jamie rested his hands on Edward's thighs. There was something strange in his eyes. Was he scared?

"It's okay. Heat of the moment and all that. Don't worry about it." Sex had driven men to do and say crazier things, he was sure of that.

"No," Jamie said. "It's not that. Just…" He cleared his throat and stepped away, fastening his pants and retrieving his shirt from the floor. "I'm not good at this." He waved a hand between them. "Talking. Sharing my feelings." He pulled on his shirt.

"It's okay," Edward assured him and sat up. He held onto the edge of the desk and looked down at the damp patch on his underwear. He didn't expect some huge declaration of love. But knowing Jamie had some feelings for him and for him to verbalize them, that meant something. He was obviously in Jamie's plans for the future.

"I do love you," Jamie blurted out.

Edward pressed his lips into a thoughtful pout and considered the Marine, or rather, the man. "Come here," he said and held out his hand. He smiled as Jamie took it and pulled the other man toward him. He placed his other hand on Jamie's chest then ran it over the scarred skin visible beneath the open shirt. With a sigh, he moved his hand higher, then wrapped it around the back of Jamie's neck and pulled him into an openmouthed kiss.

Eventually, Edward broke the kiss and lowered his head. He cared about Jamie too. Resting his forehead against Jamie's, he whispered, "I love you too." He met Jamie's relieved eyes and smiled as he kissed him again. "I do."

Epilogue

JAMIE SCOOPED UP HIS JEANS AND STUFFED THEM INTO HIS backpack. They wouldn't fit no matter how he tried to get them in.

"Here," Edward said patiently. "For an engineer who can calculate structures within inches I don't get why you can't see folding is where it's at." Edward folded the jeans, then, peering inside of the backpack, tutted and tipped the entire contents onto the bed.

"Edward—"

"Leave it to me," Edward said. Within minutes he'd repacked the bag and Jamie had to admit that everything fit with room to spare. He pulled Edward in to kiss him thank you. They'd been together nearly a year now and in all that time all Jamie wanted to do was kiss the man he'd fallen so hard for.

"I didn't see your toothbrush in there or your deodorant," Edward commented when they parted from the kiss.

Now that was a leading question. Jamie had a small room near the office of Bowyer Industries, where he worked as a lowly intern. The room was subsidized by the company and thank God it was, as property in Miami was expensive. Edward didn't really stay over. The place was tiny in comparison to the three-room apartment that Edward had over the offices of Blush Pink. Tiny and cramped.

"Jamie?" Edward prompted.

"I left them in your bathroom. With my shampoo and stuff." Jamie shrugged as he spoke.

"You want me to get them for you? There's room in the bag."

Jamie's chest tightened. Edward was so damn accommodating. He never once questioned why Jamie wouldn't just move in with him. Hell, Jamie spent most every weekend here, and nights during the week would be empty without being wrapped up in Edward's arms. Now was the time to admit things. To actually verbalize what was in his head. The worst Edward could do was tell him to leave. Taking Edward's hand he pulled him to sit on the bed next to him.

"We need to talk," Jamie started.

Edward's breath hitched. "Please don't," he whispered. Pain laced his softly spoken words. "Whatever is wrong, we can fix it."

Jamie frowned then thought about what he had said. "No. Edward, I mean…" He stopped. This was his usual inability to speak in coherent sentences when it came to deciding what his priorities were.

"Go on," Edward encouraged.

"I love you, Edward McAllister," Jamie offered. "I will always love you."

"Okay…" Edward was evidently waiting for the axe to fall and there was very real fear in his eyes.

"No, I mean, I really love you."

"And I love you. What's wrong, Jamie?"

"I'm leaving my stuff here for a reason."

"Which is?"

Jamie squirmed. "Remember what you said to me about six months ago?"

Edward's eyes widened comically. "I have a hard time remembering what I said yesterday unless I write it in my diary."

"You said I could stay here with you, invest in the apartment maybe. Make us permanent."

"I remember." Edward had a cautious look on his face.

"If you still want to, and I mean, if you've changed your mind because I left it too late and you've decided that it's not what you want, then don't be afraid to tell me. But I love you and I don't want to be apart from you and I want to stay in Miami and come home to you every night and I hope you still need me here like you said you did." There. He'd said it. Made the huge dramatic declaration of everything he wanted. Now it was Edward's turn.

Edward reached out and cupped Jamie's face with his hands. His expressive eyes were bright with emotion. Tenderly he kissed Jamie then pulled him close for a hug.

"Now," he said softly. "Stay now. Don't go back to your place tonight."

Jamie had only one answer to that really. "I'll stay."

"Stay forever." Edward smiled.

Jamie grinned. Finally everything inside him felt right. He was with a man he loved, and who loved him, and he had never been happier. He'd been given a second chance at living and he was grabbing it with both hands.

"Forever."

Read the next book in Sapphire Cay - Chase the Sun

Adam broke Scott's heart, and all he wants is a second chance for them to fall in love.

On a simple supply run to Marsh Harbor, Scott is stunned when he comes face to face with his first love. Still gorgeous, still sexy, still a liar; Scott doesn't trust Adam even after learning the full story of what happened all those years ago.

Looking for quick and easy cash, Adam got himself mixed up in the wrong crowd and paid the price – three years in prison, and he lost the one person who had ever meant anything to him. Breaking Scott's heart had been far too easy but asking for a second chance is more challenging than he could imagine.

Boyfriends for Hire

Boyfriends For Hire

1. <u>Darcy</u>
2. <u>Kaden</u>
3. Gideon
4. Jared
5. Felix
6. Caleb

Standalone Christmas

- <u>The Road to Frosty Hollow</u>

Also from RJ & Meredith

Standalone Christmas

- <u>The Road to Frosty Hollow</u>

Free Reads

- Stronger Together

Meet RJ Scott

RJ discovered romance in books at a very young age and realized that if there wasn't romance on the page, she could create it in her head. With over one hundred and fifty books published, she is a full time author of gay romance.

She lives and works out of her home in the beautiful English countryside, spends her spare time reading, watching films, and enjoying time with her family.

The last time she had a week's break from writing she didn't like it one little bit and has yet to meet a box of chocolates she couldn't defeat.

www.rjscott.co.uk | rj@rjscott.co.uk

NEWSLETTER - rjscott.co.uk/rjnews

f facebook.com/author.rjscott
instagram.com/rjscott_author
a amazon.com/author/rj-scott
BB bookbub.com/authors/rj-scott
g goodreads.com/rjscott
patreon.com/RJScott

Meet Meredith Russell

Meredith Russell lives in the heart of England. An avid fan of many story genres, she enjoys nothing less than a happy ending. She believes in heroes and romance and strives to reflect this in her writing. Sharing her imagination and passion for stories and characters is a dream Meredith is excited to turn into reality.

www.meredithrussell.co.uk
meredithrussell666@gmail.com

facebook.com/meredithrussellauthor
x.com/MeredithRAuthor
instagram.com/miss_meredith_r